William O. Stodd

Two Arrows

William O. Stoddard

Two Arrows

1st Edition | ISBN: 978-3-75242-449-2

Place of Publication: Frankfurt am Main, Germany

Year of Publication: 2020

Outlook Verlag GmbH, Germany.

Reproduction of the original.

TWO ARROWS

A STORY OF RED AND WHITE

BY

WILLIAM O. STODDARD

Chapter I

THE HUNGRY CAMP

The mountain countries of all the earth have always been wonder-lands. The oldest and best known of them are to this day full of things that nobody has found out. That is the reason why people are always exploring them, but they keep their secrets remarkably well, particularly the great secret of how they happened to get there in that shape.

The great western mountain country of the United States is made up of range after range of wonderful peaks and ridges, and men have peered in among them here and there, but for all the peering and searching nothing of the wonder to speak of has been rubbed away.

Right in the eastern, edge of one of these mountain ridges, one warm September morning, not long ago, a band of Nez Percé Indians were encamped. It was in what is commonly called "the Far West," because always when you get there the West is as far away as ever. The camp was in a sort of nook, and it was not easy to say whether a spur of the mountain jutted out into the plain, or whether a spur of the plain made a dent in the ragged line of the mountains. More than a dozen "lodges," made of skins upheld by poles, were scattered around on the smoother spots, not far from a bubbling spring of water. There were some trees and bushes and patches of grass near the spring, but the little brook which trickled away from it did not travel a great way into the world, from the place where it was born, before it was soaked up and disappeared among the sand and gravel. Up and beyond the spring, the farther one chose to look, the rockier and the ruggeder everything seemed to be.

Take it all together, it was a forlorn looking, hot, dried-up, and uncomfortable sort of place. The very lodges themselves, and the human beings around them, made it appear pitifully desolate. The spring was the only visible thing that seemed to be alive and cheerful and at work.

There were Indians and squaws to be seen, a number of them, and boys and girls of all sizes, and some of the squaws carried pappooses, but they all looked as if they had given up entirely and did not expect to live any longer. Even some of the largest men had an air of not caring much, really, whether they lived or not; but that was the only regular and dignified way for a Nez Percé or any other Indian warrior to take a thing he can't help or is too lazy to fight with. The women showed more signs of life than the men, for some of them were moving about among the children, and one poor, old, withered, ragged squaw sat in the door of her lodge, with her gray hair all down over her face, rocking backward and forward, and singing a sort of droning chant.

There was not one quadruped of any kind to be seen in or about that camp. Behind this fact was the secret of the whole matter. Those Indians were starving! Days and days before that they had been away out upon the plains to the eastward, hunting for buffalo. They had not found any, but they had found all the grass dry and parched by a long drought, so that no buffalo in his senses was likely to be there, and so that their own ponies could hardly make a living by picking all night. Then one afternoon a great swarm of locusts found where they were and alighted upon them just as a westerly wind died out. The locusts remained long enough to eat up whatever grass there was left. All through the evening the Nez Percés had heard the harsh, tingling hum of those devourers, as they argued among themselves whether or not it were best to stay and dig for the roots of the grass. The wind came up suddenly and strongly about midnight, and the locusts decided to take advantage of it and sail away after better grass, but they did not leave any behind them. They set out for the nearest white settlements in hope of getting corn and apple-tree leaves, and all that sort of thing.

The band of Nez Percés would have moved away the next morning under any circumstances, but when morning came they were in a terribly bad predicament. Not one of them carried a watch, or he might have known that it was about three o'clock, and very dark, when a worse disaster than the visit of the locusts took place. By five or six minutes past three it was all done completely, and it was the work of a wicked old mule.

All but a half a dozen of the ponies and mules of the band had been gathered and tethered in what is called a "corral," only that it had no fence, at a short distance from the lodges. Nobody dreamed of any danger to that corral, and there was none from the outside, even after the boys who were set to watch it had curled down and gone to sleep. All the danger was inside, and it was also inside of that mule. He was hungry and vicious. He had lived in the white "settlements," and knew something. He was fastened by a long hide lariat to a peg driven into the ground, as were all the others, and he knew that the best place to gnaw in two that lariat was close to the peg, where he could get a good pull upon it. As soon as he had freed himself he tried the lariat of another mule, and found that the peg had been driven into loose earth and came right up. That was a scientific discovery, and he tried several other pegs. Some came up with more or less hard tugging, and as fast as they came up a pony or a mule was free. Then he came to a peg he could not pull, and he lost his temper. He squealed, and turned around and kicked the pony that belonged to that peg. Then he stood still and brayed, as if he were frightened to find himself loose, and that was all that was needed.

It was after three o'clock, and in one minute the whole corral was kicking and squealing, braying, biting, and getting free, and joining in the general opinion that it was time to run away.

That is what the western men call a "stampede," and whenever one occurs there is pretty surely a mule or a thief at the bottom of it; but sometimes a hail-storm will do as well, or nearly so. By five or six minutes past three all of that herd were racing westward, with boys and men getting out of breath behind it, and all the squaws in the camp were holding hard upon the lariats of the ponies tethered among the lodges. When morning came there were hardly ponies enough to "pack" the lodges and other baggage and every soul of the band had to carry something as they all set off, bright and early, upon the trail of the stampeded drove of ponies. Some of the warriors had followed it without any stopping for breakfast, and they might have caught up with it, perhaps, but for the good generalship of that old mule. He had decided in his own mind to trot right along until he came to something to eat and drink, and the idea was a persuasive one. All the rest determined to have something to eat and drink, and they followed their leader. It was not easy for men on foot to catch up with them, and before noon the warriors sat down and took a smoke, and held a council as to what it was best to do. Before they finished that council the ponies had gained several miles more the start of them. The next council the warriors held contained but three men, for all the rest had gone back as messengers to tell the band that the ponies had not been recovered. By nightfall the remaining three had faithfully carried back the same news, and were ready for a fresh start.

After that there had been day after day of weary plodding and continual disappointment, with the weather growing hotter and the grass drier, until the trail they were following brought them to the spring in the edge of the mountain range without bringing them to the wicked old mule and his followers.

That had not been the whole of the sad history. On the evening before the stampede that band of Nez Percés had been well supplied with riding ponies and pack-mules, and had also been rich in dogs. No other band of their size had more, although their failure to find buffaloes had already begun to have its effect upon the number of their barking stock. Not a dog had been wasted by feeding him to the other dogs, but the human beings had not been allowed to starve, and after the march began towards the mountains there was less and less noise in that camp night after night.

There was no help for it; the ponies ate the grass up at the spring, and then one of them had to be eaten, while the warriors rode all around the neighborhood vainly hunting for something better and not so expensive. They did secure a few rabbits and sage-hens and one small antelope, but all the signs of the times grew blacker and blacker, and it was about as well to kill and eat the remaining ponies as to let them die of starvation. A sort of apathy seemed to fall upon everybody, old and young, and the warriors hardly felt like doing any more hunting. Now at last they sat down to starve, without a dog or pony left, and with no prospect that game of any kind would come into camp to be killed. It is a curious fact, but whole bands of Indians, and sometimes whole tribes, get into precisely that sort of scrape almost every year. Now it is one band, and now it is another, and there would be vastly more of it if it were not for the United States Government.

There was nothing droll, nothing funny, nothing that was not savagely sad, about the Nez Percés' camp that September morning. Every member of the band, except two, was loafing around the lodges hopelessly and helplessly doing nothing, and miserably giving the matter up.

CHAPTER II

A YOUNG HERO

Away from the camp a long mile, and down in the edge of the dry, hot, desolate plain, there was a wide spread of sage-bushes. They were larger than usual, because of having ordinarily a better supply of water sent them from the mountains than if they had settled further out. In among such growths are apt to be found sage-hens and rabbits, and sometimes antelopes, but the warriors had decided that they had hunted out all of the game that had been there, and had given the bushes up. Two of the members of the band who were not warriors had not arrived at the same conclusion, and both of these were among the "sage-brush" that morning. The first had been greatly missed among the lodges, and had been much hunted for and shouted after, for he was the largest and most intelligent dog ever owned by that band. He was also about the ugliest ever owned by anybody, and his misfortunes had earned for him the name of One-eye. He could see more with the eye he had left—and it was his right—than any other animal they had ever had, or than most of the warriors. He saw what became of the other dogs, for instance, and at once acquired a habit of not coming when an Indian called for him. He kept his eye about him all day, and was careful as to where he lay down. Just about the time when the ponies began to go into the camp-kettles he was a dog hard to find, although he managed to steal pony-bones and carry them away into the sage-brush. Perhaps it was for this reason that he was in even better condition than common that morning. He had no signs of famine about him, and he lay beside what was left of a jackass-rabbit, which he had managed to add to his stock of plunder. One-eye was a dog of uncommon sagacity; he had taken a look at the camp just before sunrise, and had confirmed his convictions that it was a bad place for him. He had been to the spring for water, drinking enough to last him a good while, and then he had made a race against time for the nearest bushes. He lay now with his sharp-pointed, wolfish ears pricked forward, listening to the tokens of another presence besides his own.

Somebody else was there, but not in bodily condition to have made much of a race after One-eye. It was a well-grown boy of about fifteen years, and One-eye at once recognized him as his own particular master, but he was a very forlorn-looking boy. He wore no clothing, except the deer-skin "clout" that covered him from above his hips to the middle of his thighs. He carried a light lance in one hand and a bow in the other, and there were arrows in the quiver slung over his shoulder. A good butcher-knife hung in its case by the thong around his waist, and he was evidently out on a hunting expedition. He was the one being, except One-eye, remaining in that band of Nez Percés, with life and energy enough to try and do something. He did not look as if he could do much. He was the son of the old chief in command of the band, but it was two whole days since he had eaten anything, and he had a faded, worn, drawn, hungry appearance, until you came to his black, brilliant eyes. These had an unusual fire in them, and glanced quickly, restlessly, piercingly in all directions. He might have been even good-looking if he had been well fed and well dressed, and he was tall and strongly built. Just such Indian boys grow up into the chiefs and leaders who make themselves famous, and get their exploits into the newspapers, but as yet this particular boy had not managed to earn for himself any name at all. Every Indian has to do something notable or have something memorable occur to him before his tribe gives him the honor of a distinguishing name. One-eye knew him, and knew that he was hungry and in trouble, but had no name for him except that he suggested a danger of the camp-kettle.

There could be no doubt about that boy's pluck and ambition, and he was a master for any dog to have been proud of as he resolutely and stealthily searched the sage-bushes. He found nothing, up to the moment when he came out into a small bit of open space, and then he suddenly stopped, for there was something facing him under the opposite bushes.

"Ugh! One-eye."

A low whine replied to him, and a wag of a dog's tail was added, but a watch was kept upon any motion he might make with his bow or lance.

"Ugh! no. Not kill him," remarked the boy, after almost a minute of profound thinking. "Eat him? No dog then. All old fools. No dog hunt with. No pony. Starve. Keep One-eye. Try for rabbits."

He called repeatedly, but his old acquaintance refused to come near him, whining a little but receding as the boy advanced.

"Ugh! knows too much."

It was a matter to lessen the value of One-eye that he understood his own interests, and his master ceased, wearily, his efforts to entice him. He pushed on through the bushes, but now he was instantly aware that One-eye was searching them with him, keeping at a safe distance, but performing regular hunter's duty. He even scared up a solitary sage-hen, but she did not fly within range of bow and arrow. She was an encouragement, however, and so were the remains of the rabbit to which One-eye managed to pilot the way. They seemed like a promise of better things to come, and One-eye stood over them for a moment wagging his tail, as much as to say,

"There; take that and let me up!"

The boy picked up the rabbit and said several things to the dog in a clear, musical voice. He spoke the guttural, Nez Percé dialect, which is one of the most difficult in the world, and One-eye seemed almost to understand him—and yet there are white boys of fifteen who stumble dreadfully over such easy tongues as Greek and Latin.

The boy and dog seemed to be on better terms after that, and went on through the sage-brush towards where a straggling line of mesquite scrubs marked the plain. The dog was ranging the bushes right and left, while the boy slowly followed the narrow lane of an old, hard-beaten "buffalo path," with an arrow on the string, ready for anything that might turn up. They were nearly out of the mesquites when One-eye uttered a quick, sharp, low-voiced whine, which his master seemed to understand. It is not every dog that can whine in the Nez Percé dialect, but the boy at once dropped upon his hands and knees and crept silently forward. He had been warned that something was the matter, and his natural instinct was to hide until he should discover what it might be. Again the dog whimpered, and the boy knew that he was hidden ahead and beyond him. He crawled out of the trail and made his way under and through the bushes. He made no more sound or disturbance than a snake would have caused in doing the same thing, and in half a minute more he was peering out into the open country.

"Ugh! buffalo!"

His brilliant eyes served him well. Only an Indian or a dog would have rightly read the meaning of some very minute variations in the brown crest of a roll of the prairie, far away to the eastward. Only the keenest vision could have detected the fact that there was a movement in the low, dull line of desolation. Back shrank the boy, under the bushes at the side of the trail, and One-eye now had enough of restored confidence to come and crouch beside him. In a few minutes more the spots were noticeably larger, and it was plain that the buffalo were approaching and not receding. At another time and under different circumstances, even an Indian might have been unwise, and have tried to creep out and meet them, but the weakness of semistarvation brought with it a most prudent suggestion. It was manifestly better to lie still and let them come, so long as they were coming. There was no sort of fatigue in such a style of hunting, but there was a vast deal of excitement. It was a strain on any nerves, especially hungry ones, to lie still while those two great shaggy shapes came slowly out upon the ridge. They did not pause for an instant, and there was no grass around them to give them an excuse for lingering. They were on their way after some, and some water, undoubtedly, and perhaps they knew a reason why there should be an ancient buffalo-trail in that direction, trodden by generation after generation of their grass-eating race. The boy was a born hunter, and knew that he was lurking in the right place, and he drew back farther and under deeper and more perfect cover, hardly seeming to breathe. One-eye did the same, had almost looked as if he wanted to put his paw over his mouth as he panted. On came the two bisons, and it was apparent soon that no more were following them.

"Bull—cow," muttered the boy. "Get both. Laugh at old men then. Have name!"

His black eyes flashed as he put his best arrow on the string and flattened himself upon the dry, hot earth. Nearer and nearer drew the gigantic game, and with steady, lumbering pace they followed the old trail. It was a breathless piece of business, but it was over at last. The bull was in front, and he was a splendid-looking old fellow, although somewhat thin in flesh. Neither he nor his companion seemed to have smelled or dreamed of danger, and they walked straight into it. The moment for action had come, and the boy's body rose a little, with a swift, pliant, graceful motion. With all the strength starvation had left in him he drew his arrow to the head. In another second it was buried to its very feathers in the broad breast of the buffalo bull, and the great animal stumbled forward upon his knees, pierced through the heart. The young hunter had known well the precise spot to aim at, and he had made a perfect shot. The cow halted for a moment, as if in amazement, and then charged forward along the trail. That moment had given the boy enough time to put another arrow on the string, and as she passed him he drove it into her just behind the shoulder, well and vigorously. Once more he had given a deadly wound, and now he caught up his lance. There was little need of it, but he could not be sure of that, and so, as the bull staggered to his feet in his death-struggle, he received a terrific thrust in the side and went down again. It was a complete victory, so far as the bull was concerned, and One-eye had darted away upon the path of the wounded cow.

"Ugh! got both!" exclaimed the boy. "Have name now."

Chapter III

A BRAVE NAME

One-eye followed the arrow-stricken cow, and he ran well. So did the cow, and she did not turn to the right or left from the old buffalo trail. There was but one road for either the trail or the cow or the dog, for the very formation of the land led them all into the mountains through the nook by the spring, and so by and by through the camp of the starving Nez Percés. On she went until, right in the middle of the camp and among the lodges, she stumbled and fell, and One-eye had her by the throat.

It was time for somebody to wake up and do something, and a wiry-looking, undersized, lean-ribbed old warrior, with an immense head, whose bow and arrows had been hanging near him, at once rushed forward and began to make a sort of pin-cushion of that cow. He twanged arrow after arrow into her, yelling ferociously, and was just turning away to get his lance when a robust squaw, who had not been made very thin even by starvation, caught him by the arm, screeching,

"Dead five times! What for kill any more?"

She held up a plump hand as she spoke, and spread her brown fingers almost against his nose. There was no denying it, but the victorious hunter at once struck an attitude and exclaimed,

"No starve now, Big Tongue!"

He had saved the whole band from ruin and he went on to say as much, while the warriors and squaws and smaller Indians crowded around the game so wonderfully brought within a few yards of their kettles. It was a grand occasion, and the Big Tongue was entitled to the everlasting gratitude of his nation quite as much as are a great many white statesmen and kings and generals who claim and in a manner get it. All went well with him until a gray-headed old warrior, who was examining the several arrows projecting from the side of the dead bison, came to one over which he paused thoughtfully. Then he raised his head, put his hand to his mouth, and sent forth a wild whoop of delight. He drew out the arrow with one sharp tug and held it up to the gaze of all.

"Not Big Tongue. Boy!" For he was the father of the young hero who had faithfully stood up against hunger and despair and had gone for game to the very last. He was a proud old chief and father that day, and all that was left for the Big Tongue was to recover his own arrows as fast as he could for future use, while the squaws cut up the cow. They did it with a haste and skill quite remarkable, considering how nearly dead they all were. The prospect of a good dinner seemed to put new life into them, and they plied their knives in half a dozen places at the same time.

One-eye sat down and howled for a moment, and then started off upon the trail by which he had come.

"Boy!" shouted the old chief. "All come. See what."

Several braves and nearly all the other boys, one squaw and four half-grown girls at once followed him as he pursued the retreating form of One-eye. It was quite a procession, but some of its members staggered a little in their walk, and there was no running. Even the excitement of the moment could get no more than a rapid stride out of the old chief himself. He was well in advance of all others, and at the edge of the expanse of sage-brush in which One-eye disappeared he was compelled to pause for breath. Before it had fully come to him he needed it for another whoop of delight.

Along the path in front of him, erect and proud, but using the shaft of his lance as a walking-stick, came his own triumphant boy hunter. Not one word did the youngster utter, but he silently turned in his tracks, beckoning his father to follow.

It was but a few minutes after that and they stood together in front of the dead bull bison. The boy pointed at the arrow almost buried in the shaggy chest, and then he sat down; hunger and fatigue and excitement had done their work upon him, and he could keep his feet no longer. He even permitted One-eye to lick his hands and face in a way no Indian dog is in the habit of doing. Other warriors came crowding around the great trophy, and the old chief waited while they examined all and made their remarks. They were needed as witnesses of the exact state of affairs, and they all testified that this arrow, like the other, had been wonderfully well driven. The old chief sat down before the bull and slowly pulled out the weapon. He looked at it, held it up, streaming with the blood of the animal it had brought down, and said:

"Long Bear is a great chief. Great brave. Tell all people the young chief Two ARROWS. Boy got a name. Whoop!"

The youngster was on his feet in a moment, and One-eye gave a sharp, fierce bark, as if he also was aware that something great had happened and that he had a share in it. It was glory enough for one day, and the next duty on hand was to repair the damages of their long fasting. Two Arrows and his dog walked proudly at the side of the Long Bear as he led the way back to the camp. No longer a nameless boy, he was still only in his apprenticeship; he was not yet a warrior, although almost to be counted as a "brave," as his title indicated. It would yet be a long time before he could be permitted to go upon any war-path, however he might be assured of a good pony when there should be hunting to be done.

There had been all along an abundance of firewood, of fallen trees and dead mesquite-bushes, in the neighborhood of the camp, and there were fires burning in front of several lodges before the remainder of the good news came in. The cow had been thoroughly cut up, but the stern requirements of Indian law in such cases called for the presence of the chief and the leading warriors to divide and give out for use. Anything like theft or overreaching would have been visited with the sharp wrath of some very hungry men. The Big Tongue had seated himself in front of the "hump" and some other choice morsels, waiting the expected decision that they belonged to him. He also explained to all who could not help hearing him how surely that cow could have broken through the camp and escaped into the mountains if it had not been for him, until the same plump squaw pointed at the hump and ribs before him, remarking, cheerfully,

"Go get arrow. Kill him again. Need some more. Boy kill him when he stood up."

There was not strength left in the camp for a laugh, but the Big Tongue seemed to have wearied of the conversation. He looked wearier afterwards when the hump was unanimously assigned to the old chief's own lodge, that Two Arrows might eat his share of it. Indian justice is a pretty fair article when it can be had at home, not interfered with by any kind of white man. The division was made to the entire satisfaction of everybody, after all, for the Big Tongue deserved and was awarded due credit and pay for his promptness. If the buffalo had not already been killed by somebody else, perhaps he might have killed it, and there was a good deal in that. He and his family had a very much encouraged and cheerful set of brown faces as they gathered around their fire and began to broil bits of meat over it.

One fashion was absolutely without an exception, leaving out of the question the smaller pappooses: not one man, woman, or child but was diligently working away at a slice of raw meat, whatever else they were doing or trying to do. It was no time to wait for cookery, and it was wonderful what an enlivening effect the raw meat seemed to have.

Indian etiquette required that Two Arrows should sit down before his father's lodge and patiently wait until his "token" should be given him. His first slice of meat was duly broiled by his mother, and handed him by his father, and he ate it in dignified silence. It was the proudest hour of his whole life thus far, and he well knew that the story would spread through the Nez Percé nation and lead the old men of it to expect great things of him: it was a beginning of fame, and it kindled in him a tremendous fever for more. His ambition grew and grew as his appetite went down, and his strength began to come back to him.

It was a grand feast, and it was not long before there were braves and squaws ready to go and cut up the bull and bring every ounce of him to camp. Starvation had been defeated, and all that happiness had been earned by "Two Arrows."

Chapter IV

THE MINING EXPEDITION

The place away out upon the rolling plain, at which the unlucky hunting-camp of the Nez Percé band had been pitched when the locusts visited them, was occupied again a few days after they left it. The new-comers were not Indians of any tribe but genuine white men, with an uncommonly good outfit for a small one. They were one of the hundreds of mining and exploring expeditions which every year set out for one range of mountains or another to try and find what there is in them. They are all sure to find a good deal of hard work, privation and danger, and some of them discover mines of gold and silver.

This expedition consisted of two very strongly built but not heavy wagons, with canvas-covered tilts, and each drawn by four large mules. What was in the wagons except the drivers could only be guessed at, but riding at the side or ahead or behind them as they came towards the camping-place were six men and a boy. There were several spare horses and mules, and the whole affair looked as if it had cost a good deal of money. It costs a great deal to bring up eight men and a boy so that these may be fairly included, but there were wide variations in the external garnishing of the riders and drivers.

They had all been guided to that spot, partly by the general aim of their undertaking, partly by the trail they were following, and a good deal by a tall old fellow with a Roman nose and a long, muddy yellow beard, who rode in front upon a raw-boned, Roman-nosed sorrel mare, with an uncommon allowance of tail. When they reached that camping-ground it was not late in the afternoon, but it was not well to go on past a deep pool of water, surrounded by willows and cottonwood-trees, however little grass there was to be had in the neighborhood. They had found water and grass getting scarcer and scarcer for two or three days, and there was quite enough in the look of things to make men thoughtful. They knew nothing about the Nez Percés and the grasshoppers and the wicked old mule, but the tall man in front only looked around for one moment before he exclaimed,

"I'd call it—Been some kind of Injins here lately. No game, I reckon, or they'd ha' stayed."

"No kind of game'd stay long in such a burned-up country as this is," added a squarely made, gray-headed man who rode up alongside of him. "We've nothing to do but to push on. We must get out of this or we'll lose our whole outfit."

"Sure as shootin'! I move we just unhitch long enough for a feed and a good drink, and lay in what water we can carry, and go on all night. There's a good moon to travel by, and it'll be cooler work for the critters."

"It's our best hold. Sile, don't you gallop that horse of yours one rod. There's work enough before him. Save him up."

"All right, father. But isn't this the camp? He can rest now."

"No he can't, nor you either. It's an all-night job."

Sile was not gray-headed. He was very nearly red-headed. Still, he looked enough like his father in several ways. He was broadly and heavily built, strong and hearty, with something in his merry, freckled face which seemed to indicate a very good opinion of himself. Boys of fourteen, or thereabout, who can ride and shoot, and who have travelled a little, are apt to get that kind of expression, and it never tells lies about them.

Sile's horse was a roan, and looked like a fast one under a light weight like his. Just large enough not to be called "ponyish," and with signs of high spirit. The moment the youngster sprang from the saddle and began to remove it it became manifest that there was a good understanding between horse and boy. Any intelligent animal is inclined to make a pet of its master if it has a fair chance.

"Now, Hip, there isn't any grass, but you can make believe. I'll bring a nose-bag as soon as you've cooled off and have had a drink of water."

He was as good as his word, and there were oats in the nose-bag when he brought it, and Hip shortly left it empty, but in less than two hours from that time the two tilted wagons were once more moving steadily onward towards the West and the mountains.

There had been a hearty supper cooked and eaten, and there was not a human being in the party who seemed much the worse for fatigue. The spare horses and mules had taken the places of the first lot in harness, and it was plain that there was plenty of working power remaining, but there was a sort of serious air about the whole matter. The sun set after a while, and still, with occasional brief rests, the expedition pushed forward. It was a point to be noted that it travelled about twice as fast as the band of Nez Percés had been able to do after they had lost their ponies. It was not hampered by any heavily burdened foot-passengers. The moon arose, and now Sile was riding on in front with the muddy-bearded veteran.

"Pine," said he, "s'pose we don't come to grass and water?"

"Most likely we will before mornin', or before noon anyhow. If we don't, we must go on till we do."

"Kill all the mules?"

"They'll all die if we don't, sure's my name's Pine—Yellow Pine."

"They can't stand it—"

"They can stand anything but starvation. Did you ever try giving up water?"

"No; did you?"

"Well, I did. I was glad to give up giving it up after a few days. It's the queerest feeling you ever had."

"How'd it happen?"

"I don't feel like tellin' about it jest now. There's too good a chance for tryin' it again to suit me."

"Is that so? Pine, do you know, I wish you'd tell me how they came to call you Yellow Pine."

The fear of either thirst or hunger had plainly not yet fallen upon Sile, or he would not have asked that question just then. It sounded so much like fourteen years old and recklessness that the great, gaunt man turned in his saddle and looked at him.

"I'd call it—Well, now, you're a customer. Some reckon it's my complexion, and I am turned kind o' yaller, but it ain't. It's my own name."

"How'd you get it, anyway?"

"How? Well, my father was just like me; he was a wise man. He named me after his brother, my uncle Ogden, and after Colonel Yell, that was killed in the Mexican war. So I'm Yell O. Pine, and nobody but you ever cared how it kem so."

Sile was satisfied as to that one point, but there did not seem to be anything else on that prairie about which he was satisfied, and at last his companion remarked to him,

"Now look here, Sile Parks, you go back and tell the judge, if I've got to answer questions for you all night, he'll hev to raise my wages. I'm thirsty with it now, and there's no water to spare."

Sile was in no wise disconcerted, but rode back to the main body in excellent spirits. It was the first real danger of any sort that the expedition had encountered, and there was a keen excitement in it. He had read of such things, and now he was in one without the least idea in the world but what everything would come out all right, just as it does in a novel. Before midnight he had asked every other human being around him all the questions he could think of, and had dismounted four times to examine the grass at the wayside and see if it were of any better quality. Each time he was compelled to mount again and ride on to his father, "Chips."

When bunch-grass gets to be so dry that it will crumble in the fingers it ceases to be of any use except to carry a prairie-fire in a great hurry. It will do that wonderfully, but it will not do to feed animals on, and it was needful to have something better.

When a halt was called, at about twelve o'clock, and a rest of two hours was decided on, the barrels of water in the wagons were drawn upon for only a moderate ration all around, and the animals plainly testified their eagerness for more. They were not at all distressed as yet, but they would have been if they had done that amount of work under sunshine. When the moment for again setting out arrived and the word was given, Judge Parks inquired,

"Pine, where is Sile?"

"Where? I'd call it—There he is on his blanket, sound asleep. I'll shake him up."

"Do, while I put the saddle on his horse. Guess he's tired a little."

A sharp shake of Sile's shoulder had to be followed by another, and then a sleepy voice responded,

"Water? Why, Pine, there's a whole lake of it. Was you ever at sea?"

"Sea be hanged! Git up; it's time to travel."

"Ah, halloo! I'm ready. I dreamed we'd got there. Riding so much makes me sleepy."

He was quickly in the saddle again, and they went forward; but there were long faces among them at about breakfast-time that morning. They were halted by some clumps of sickly willows, and Yellow Pine said, mournfully,

"Yer's where the redskins made their next camp. They and their critters trod the pool down to nothin' and let the sun in onto it, and it's as dry as a bone. We're in for a hard time and no mistake."

CHAPTER V

A VERY OLD TRAIL

During all that was left of that happy day in the Nez Percé camp there was an immense amount of broiling and boiling done. Whoever left the great business of eating enough and went and sat down or lay down got up again after a while and did some more remarkable eating. All the life of an Indian trains him for that kind of thing, for he goes on in a sort of continual vibration from feast to famine.

All the other boys in camp were as hungry as Two Arrows, and as their hunger went down their envy of him went up; he had suddenly stepped ahead of them and had become an older boy in a moment. It was very much as if a boy of his age in the "settlements" had waked up, some fine morning, with a pair of mustaches and a military title, uniform and all.

Two Arrows was entitled to strut a little, and so was One-eye, but for some reason neither of them was inclined to anything but eating and lying down. One-eye may have felt lonely, for he found himself the only dog in all that camp, and he knew very well what had become of the dogs he used to know: they had gone to the famine, and there had been no sort of funeral ceremonies, and now there could be no kind of neighborly quarrel over bones any more. There was a reason, why One-eye should attach himself more closely than ever to his master and follow his every movement. They had killed two buffaloes in company, and there was no telling what they might or might not yet do if they kept together.

Two Arrows found the effects of his long fasting rapidly passing away, but he was like everybody else and needed a big sleep. One-eye had the only eye that did any watching all that night, and nobody but the fat squaw was up very early next morning. Her next company was the Big Tongue, and he at once began to talk about the game he intended to kill, now he had had something to eat. Two Arrows might not have been the next riser if it had not been for a friendly tug from One-eye, but the moment he was awake he knew that he was hungry again. He was hungry, but he was silent, and it was plain that he was thinking about something uncommonly interesting. He stood in front of his father's lodge, waiting for the breakfast that was now sure to come, when a light hand was laid upon his arm and a soft musical voice exclaimed, triumphantly,

"Two Arrows! Name!"

"Ugh," said he. "Na-tee-kah."

He hardly looked around, but the pleasantest face in all that band was smiling upon him. It bore a strong resemblance to his own, and belonged to an Indian girl a year or so younger than himself. She was well grown, slender, and graceful, and had a pair of eyes as brilliant as his, but a great deal more gentle and kindly in their expression. They lacked the restless, searching, eager look, and his, indeed were quieter than they had been the day before.

"Got plenty to eat now," she said. "Not starve to death any more."

"Eat all up," replied he. "Fool! Starve again, pretty soon."

"No, Long Bear and old men say, keep all there is left. Work to-day. Dry meat. Go hunting somewhere else. Not stay here."

There was a little more talk that indicated a very fair degree of affection between the brother and sister, and then Two Arrows said to her,

"Keep tongue very still. Come."

She followed him to the lower edge of the camp, and he silently pointed her to the place where the old buffalo trail came in.

"Great many make that. Long time. All know why."

"The cow came in there."

"Ugh! now come."

She followed him now to the upper end of the camp, and he pointed again to the trail, deeply and plainly made, going on into the gorges of the mountains.

"Buffalo go that way; Two Arrows follow. Say no word. Not find him pretty soon."

That was the meaning of all his thoughtfulness. He meant to set off on a hunt of his own planning, without asking permission of anybody. Two days earlier he would not have dreamed of such a piece of insubordination. Now he had won his right to do that very thing, and he meant to take advantage of it instantly. All the young ambition in him had been stirred to the boiling point, and his only remaining anxiety was to get a good supply of provisions and get out of the camp without being seen by anybody. He could look out for his weapons, including several of his father's best arrows, and Na-tee-kah at once promised to steal for him all the meat he wanted. She went right into his plan with the most sisterly devotion, and her eyes looked more and more like his when she next joined her mother and the other squaws at their camp-fire. There was no doubt but what her brother would have his marching rations supplied well, and of the best that was to be had.

There was no need for Two Arrows to steal from Long Bear. What between pride and buffalo meat the old chief was ready to give or rather lend him anything, and he deemed it his heroic son's day to parade and show off. He was entitled to do so with the best weapons in his father's collection. The day would surely come when he would be allowed to paint himself and do a great many other things belonging to full-grown braves and warriors. It was even lawful for him to wear a patch or two of paint now, and Na-tee-kah helped him to put it on. If he had been a white boy with his first standing-collar, he could not have been more particular, and every other boy in camp had something to say to the others about the fit of that vermilion.

It was a day of drying and smoking meat, and of eating as much as the older men permitted, and everybody wore an aspect of extreme good-humor except One-eye and his master. The dog and the boy alike kept away from the camp-fires and from all grown-up Indians. Towards the middle of the afternoon, Na-tee-kah slipped quietly out at the upper end of the camp, carrying her own buckskin sack nearly full of something, and nobody thought of asking her what there might be in it. She had not been gone many minutes before anybody loafing at that end of the camp might have seen her brother was following her. He had been standing near the spring for some time, in full rig, for the other boys to admire him, and now he walked dignifiedly away as if he were weary of being looked at. Half a mile farther up the rugged valley he caught up with Na-tee-kah, and she returned to camp without her bead-worked sack. There was nothing at all noticeable in the whole affair, unless some suspicious person had been closely watching them. It was after sunset before there was any special inquiry for Two Arrows, and it was dark before Na-tee-kah expressed her belief that he had "gone hunt." She replied freely to every question asked her, well knowing that there would be no pursuit, but she was more than a little relieved when the old chief, instead of getting angry about it, swelled up proudly and remarked,

"Two Arrows! young brave. All like father, some day. Kill more buffalo."

Then Na-tee-kah felt courage to speak about the trail and her brother's reasoning as to where it might lead to. She had her ears boxed for that, as it had a sound of giving advice to her elders, but it was not long before her father gravely informed a circle of the warriors and braves that the path pointed out by the buffalo cow was the one by which they must seek for more like her. It was very easy to convince them that they could do nothing upon the dry, sunburnt plains, or by staying to starve again in that camp. The objection made by Big Tongue that nobody knew where that old trail might carry them was met by Long Bear conclusively. He picked up a dry pony-bone that lay on the ground and held it out to Big Tongue.

"All other trail go this way. Know all about it. Been there."

It was enough. It was better to follow an unknown trail than to starve, and it was not long before it leaked out that Two Arrows was believed to have gone ahead of them on that very road.

Precisely how far he had gone nobody had any idea. They would hardly have believed if he had sent back word, for he had travelled most diligently. There were no longer any traces of starvation about him, except that he carried no superfluous weight of flesh. He had load enough, what with his provisions and his weapons, but he did not seem to mind it. He tramped right along, with a steady, springy step, which told a good deal of his desire to get as far away from camp as he could before his absence should be discovered.

For a little distance he had found the trail rising gently with the land. Then it turned to the left and went up and over a rocky hill, and then it turned to the right again, and just about sunset it looked for all the world as if it were running right into the side of a great precipice of the mountain range. The light of the sinking sun fell clearly and brightly upon the grand masses of quartz and granite rocks, and showed him the very point where the pathway seemed to end. It looked so, but Two Arrows knew that you cannot cut off the end of a buffalo path in that way, and he pushed on, every moment finding the way steeper and more winding. He could not make any "short cuts" over such ground as that, and every Indian boy knows a fact which the white engineers of the Pacific Railway found out for themselves—that is, that a herd of buffaloes will always find the best passes through mountain ranges, and then they will go over them by the best and easiest grades. Only by bridging a chasm, or blasting rocks, or by much digging, did the railway men ever improve upon the paths pointed out by the bisons.

Two Arrows had carefully marked his point, and just as the last rays of daylight were leaving him he sat down to rest in the mouth of what was little better than a wide "notch" in the side of the vast barrier.

"Ugh! pass," he said.

Chapter VI

A THIRSTY MARCH

That was a hard day's toil for the mining expedition. It was the second day of feasting by the Nez Percés upon the game won by Two Arrows, but there was no feasting done by Judge Parks and his men. Even Sile had no more questions to ask, and at nightfall their scanty supply of water was nearly gone. Every old watercourse and even "tow-heads" of dying bushes that they came to did but each give them another disappointment. The animals were holding out well, with frequent rests, for they had been taken care of even at the expense of the human beings.

Just before sunset, as they were plodding wearily along, Yellow Pine drew his rein, turned in his saddle, and pointed away across the plain in advance and to the right of them, exclaiming,

"Redskins!"

There was no mistake about it. In a few minutes more a pretty long line of pony-riders could be seen travelling steadily southward.

"Will they attack us, father?"

"I guess not. We are too strong, even if they were hostile."

"They won't make any muss," said Pine, confidently, as he again rode forward. "There's only some two dozen on 'em, and it isn't a good time for a fight."

It was evident that the two lines of travel, crossing each other at right angles, would bring the white and red men pretty near each other, and the latter even went out of their way to have it so. Sile all but forgot how thirsty he was when the train approached the straggling array of lances, and a bare-headed warrior rode out to meet Yellow Pine. The Roman-nosed sorrel mare sniffed at the pony as if she would have preferred a bucket of water, and the two riders held out their hands.

"How?" said Pine.

"Ugh! bad. No water. How?"

A significant motion of his hand towards his mouth accompanied the response, and Pine made one like it. Then he pointed at the wagons, and again towards the west, and made motions as if he were digging. The Indian understood, and nodded and pointed at himself:

"Ugh! Kiowa."

He made a motion as if pulling a bow, pointed southward and pretended to drink something, but when he turned his finger towards the west he shook his head.

"How?" said Pine again, and the two shook hands and all the Kiowas rode on as if they were in a hurry.

"That's a pretty bad report," said Pine to Judge Parks, and Sile muttered to himself:

"Why, he hardly uttered a word."

"What does he say?" asked his father.

"Worst kind," said Pine. "He says they have been hunting northerly for several weeks. Little game, and the drought driving it all away. He doubts if we find any water between here and the mountains. Hopes to reach it by to-morrow night in the direction he's taking. The rest of his band are down there now."

"Did he say all that?" exclaimed Sile in amazement.

"You wasn't a-watchin' of him. I told him what I thought about it and what we meant to do. Tell you what, my boy, if you're to meet many redskins you've got to learn sign language. It beats words all holler."

"Well, I did see his hands and yours a-going."

"Yes, and his face and mine too, and elbows and legs. It's as easy as fallin' off a log when you once get the hang of it."

"What do you think we had better do after that?" asked Judge Parks.

"Read our own signs. Push on for water till we get some. It can't be more'n one day, now. I know just about where I am. Risk my life on it."

So they went forward, but that night had to be taken for rest and the morning found men and horses in a terrible plight. Not one drop of water had they left, and all they had been able to do for the horses and mules had been to sponge their parched mouths. They had camped near some trees and bushes, as usual, and it was just about daylight that Yellow Pine came to wake up his employer.

"Look a' here, jedge. I was too much played out to find it last night, but here it is. Come."

"Well, what is it?" asked the judge, a moment later.

Yellow Pine was pointing at a broad, deeply trodden, flinty looking rut in the surface of the prairie.

"That's the old bufler path I follered last year, when I went into the mountains, or I'm the worst sold man you ever saw. It led me jest to where we all want to go, 'zackly as I told you."

"We'd better hitch up and follow it now, then."

"We had. It'll take us west on a bee-line, and it'll go to all the chances for water there are."

The buffaloes could safely be trusted for that, and before the sun was up the mining party was following the very path which had led the big game within reach of Two Arrows and One-eye. It was less than two hours afterwards, without anybody to carry a report of it to anybody else, that the whole Nez Percé camp disappeared, and all its human occupants also took the advice of the buffaloes. It was necessary to carry all the meat they had, and all the pappooses, and a number of other things, and so it had not been possible to take all the lodges with their lodge-poles. Two of the smaller and lighter found bearers, but there were not squaws enough for the rest, and a sort of hiding-place was made for them among the rocks until they could be sent for. Indians on a journey load their ponies first, then their squaws, then the boys, but never a "brave" unless it is a matter of life and death. A warrior would as soon work for a living as carry a burden. It never takes long to break up an Indian hunting-camp, for there are no carpets or stoves or beds or pianos, and the band of Long Bear was on its way after Two Arrows and his dog in remarkably short order.

Judge Parks and his men and all his outfit would have travelled better and more cheerfully if they could have set out from beside a good spring of water. As it was, the best they could do was to dream of finding one before they should try to sleep again.

"Father," said Sile, at about twelve o'clock, "are we to stop anywhere for dinner? I'm getting husky."

"So is everybody. Imitate old Pine; he's chewing something."

"All the men have stopped chewing tobacco; they say it makes 'em thirstier."

"Of course it does. Try a chip or a piece of leather or a bit of meat—not salt meat."

"There isn't anything else."

"The less we eat the better, till we get something to drink."

"We'll all die, at this rate."

"Stand it through, my boy. I hope Pine is right about his trail and where it leads to."

He seemed confident enough about it, at any rate, and he and his Roman-nosed mare kept their place steadily at the head of the little column. So he was always the first to examine a hole or a hollow and look back and shake his head to let the rest know that it contained no water.

The sun seemed to shine hotter and hotter, and not a living creature made its appearance upon the dry and desolate plain. Away in the western horizon, at last, some dim and cloud-like irregularities began to show themselves, and Sile urged his weary horse to the side of his father, pointing at them.

"Will there be some rain?" he asked, in a dry and husky whisper.

"My poor boy! are you so thirsty as that? Those are the mountains."

Sile's mind distinctly connected the idea of mountains with that of water, and he took off his hat and swung it, vainly trying to hurrah.

"They're a long way off yet, but we can get there. Old Pine is right."

It was wonderfully good news, but every man had been allowed to gather it for himself. Nobody cared to say an unnecessary word to anybody else. It was impossible to tell the horses, and the poor brutes were suffering painfully.

"I reckon they'll hold out," said Pine; "but they'll only jest do it. We're making the tightest kind of a squeeze."

So they were, and it grew tighter and tighter as they went on. Sile managed finally to get up to Yellow Pine in the advance, and whisper,

"Were you ever any thirstier than this in all your life?"

"Yes, sir! This isn't much. Wait till you know yer tongue's a-turnin' to a dry sponge and there's coals of fire on the back of yer neck. Keep your courage up, my boy."

Sile had done so. His father had said a good deal to him about the pluck with which young Indians endured that sort of thing, and he had determined to show "Indian blood," as if he had some in him. It was the hardest kind of hard work, and it kept him all the while thinking of rivers and lakes and ice and even lemonade. At last he saw a sage-hen, and he said to Pine,

"Isn't that a sign of water?"

"Them things never drink," said Pine "When you come to eat 'em they need to be b'iled twice. They're jest the driest bird there is. There's the mountains, though."

“Oh dear me!” groaned Sile. “But they’re getting bigger, and perhaps we’ll reach ‘em some time.”

Chapter VII

THE GREAT CAÑON

It was not yet dark when Two Arrows and One-eye halted at the mouth of the pass. One-eye looked forward and whined, but his master looked back and thought the matter over. He had travelled well and over some pretty rough ground, but the trail had been wide and well marked. It was almost like a road, so far as room went, but Two Arrows knew nothing of wheels, neither did that trail. He was considering the curious fact that not a man of his band knew that such a path existed or where it led to. It was something to set his ambition on fire only to have discovered and followed anything so new and remarkable. It was a deed for an old brave rather than for a boy of fifteen. He needed rest, but when he again turned and looked into the pass he at once arose and walked on.

"Dark soon. Maybe can't walk then. Do some more before that," said Two Arrows.

He was in a spot worth looking at. Some old-time convulsion of nature had cleft the mountain barrier at that place so that giant walls of rock arose on either side of him for hundreds of feet, almost perpendicularly. For some distance ahead the cleft was nearly straight, and its gravelly bottom was from ten to thirty yards wide. There were not many rocky fragments or bowlders, but it was evident that at some seasons of the year torrents of water came pouring through that gorge to keep it clean.

"When snow melts," muttered Two Arrows, "pretty bad place."

No doubt, or after any great storm or "cloud-burst" among the peaks beyond; but all was dry as a bone now. It was sure to become dark early in such a chasm as that, and there was no telling how much need there might be for seeing the way. On went the young explorer until he came to a point where the chasm suddenly widened. It was a gloomy sort of hollow and littered with fragments of trees, drift-wood of old torrents.

"Camp," said Two Arrows to One-eye. "Make fire."

If a dog could use flint and steel, no doubt One-eye would have obeyed; as it was, Two Arrows had to attend to that business for himself, and it was not long before a great blazing fire of mountain pine was throwing flashes of magnificent light upon the mighty precipices in all directions. The gray granite stood out like shadows, and the white quartz glittered marvellously, but the Nez Percé boy had no time to admire them. He had his supper to cook and eat, and he had found some water in a hollow of the rocks; no sunshine hot enough to dry it up had ever found its way down there. Then drift-wood was gathered to keep some sort of a blaze burning all night. There was no danger from human enemies in that utter solitude, but there were wild beasts among the mountains; night would be their prowling-time, and not one among them would venture too near a fire.

Two Arrows was well entitled to a sound sleep, and he had one; when he awoke, in the earliest gray of the next morning, the world was in fair daylight everywhere outside of that deep crack in the mountains. He ate heartily and at once pushed on, determined to have some fresh game before night if possible. Such thoughts as he sent back to the Nez Percé camp did not include the idea that it was already breaking up to follow him; still less did he have any imagination of thirsty white people toiling across a waterless plain along that buffalo trail.

He was in no danger of losing the way, for his path was walled in for him. Towards midday it ceased to go up, up, up, and the chasm widened into a great rocky cañon of wonderful ruggedness and beauty. Two Arrows had been among the mountains before, in other ranges, and this seemed to him very much like what he might have expected. Now, however, the trail turned to the right and picked its way along the steep side of the varying slopes. Here it was wider and there it was narrower, until it came to a reach of natural roadway that even a bison must have hunted for before he found it. Away up it went in zigzags, seeming to take skilful advantage of every natural help it came to, and then it shot along the mountain-side for a thousand feet, traversing a mere ledge, where one formation of rock projected out below another and made a shelf for it to go upon. If a man had fallen from that shelf he would have gone down a tremendous depth upon jagged rocks at the bottom of the cañon.

Two Arrows wasted no time in useless observations or admiration. Where herd after herd of wild cattle had tramped before him he could surely follow, and at the end of that ledge the road began to descend. The descent was gradual, and uncommonly free from breakages. It led, before a great while, once more to the bottom of the gorge. Several times Two Arrows saw "big-horn" or Rocky Mountain sheep among the rocks above him, far out of the reach of his arrows. He felt a longing for antelope venison, but there was no use in trying to catch one of those fellows. Hotter than anything else he felt the fever and fire of his ambition, stirring him to push on and do more than he had ever heard of as done by any other boy of his age among all the bands of his nation. It made him walk fast and firmly in the bracing mountain air, and he drew his breath somewhat quickly at times, when he thought of the wonderful things which might be before him. He had no watch, but just as the sun stood nearly over his head, or, rather, over the middle of the great gorge, he could see that this was beginning to grow broader and not so steep. It was promising to lead out into something, and One-eye dashed on ahead as if to ascertain what it might be. Two Arrows stood still for a moment and watched him, and then he started as if something had pricked him. The dog was crouching and creeping as if he had his remaining eye upon game of some sort or on danger. His master also crouched and crept, slipping forward rapidly from rock to rock. In three minutes more he lay beside One-eye, and they both had something worth while to look at. Not more than three hundred yards beyond them, on the crest of a rocky ledge that came out from the mountain-side like an abutment, stood a big-horn antelope. He had seen One-eye and was looking at him. He may have been studying whether or not it could be needful for an antelope away up where he was to spring away any farther from a dog and an Indian boy. He had better have been looking behind him and above him, for his real danger was not in the quiver of Two Arrows; it was crouching upon a higher fragment of the very ledge which held him, and it was preparing for immediate action. It was a cougar, or American panther, of full size, on the watch for antelopes, and now had crept almost within springing distance. Two Arrows laid his hand upon the head of One-eye to keep him silent, and watched breathlessly to see the end of that hunting. Nearer and nearer crept the cougar, and still the big-horn was absorbed in his study of matters down below. He stepped forward to the very edge, and below him the rock came down with a perpendicular face of a hundred feet. There was no danger that he would grow dizzy, but even the cougar would have done wisely to have ascertained beforehand the precise nature of the trap set for him. As it was, he gathered his lithe and graceful form for his leap, every muscle quivering with eagerness, and he put all his strength into one great, splendid bound. It was as sure as a rifle-shot, and it landed him upon the shoulders of the big-horn. He had seized his prize, but he had done too much: he had fallen with a weight and force which sent him and his antelope irresistibly over the rocky edge, and down, down, down they came together with a great thud upon the granite below.

"Whoop!" The voice of Two Arrows ringing through the gorge was joined by the fierce bark of One-eye as they sprang forward. An older warrior might have waited to know the effect of that fall before he interfered between a cougar and his game, but Two Arrows did not think of hesitation. It was just as well. What between the blow of the cougar and the force of the fall, the big-horn was dead. He had somewhat broken the effect of the terrible shock upon his enemy by falling under him, but even the tough body of the great "cat o' mountain" had not been made for such plunges, and he lay on the rock stunned and temporarily disabled. Whether it would, after all, have killed him, he was never to know, for, just as he was staggering to his feet, a Nez Percé Indian boy charged upon him with a long lance, while a large and ambitious dog rushed in and seized him by the throat. He was taken at an advantage.

Thrust, thrust, thrust, in fiercely rapid succession, came the keen blade of the lance, and One-eye bore down and throttled a brute that could have killed four such dogs in anything like a fair fight.

It was tremendous hunting for a boy of fifteen. A cougar to bring down his antelope for him, and a precipice to help him kill his cougar, and only just enough work for his lance and dog to entitle him to the honor of closing, single-handed, with one of the most dangerous of wild animals. He had done that very thing, nevertheless, and was entitled to all the credit of it. If he had waited to consider the matter, he might have had a much harder fight for it. What was more, his energy and enterprise and endurance had resulted in bringing him to the right place at the right time, instead of somewhere else.

Chapter VIII

WATER! WATER!

By the time the band of Nez Percés was well on its way, the Big Tongue had persuaded himself that the movement was in large part a following of his own advice. He felt very free to say as much in the presence of several squaws. He even ruffled up and looked large when Na-tee-kah laughed and turned away her head. She was too young to say anything in reply to a grown-up brave, but just behind her was the fat squaw, and her tongue was habitually more at liberty.

"Kill cow same way," said she. "Two Arrows kill him first; then Big Tongue. Great brave!"

Big Tongue turned upon her almost fiercely, exclaiming.

"Squaw no talk!"

"Big Tongue keep still. Squaw-boy beat him. Big Tongue shoot arrows into dead cow. Ha-ha-pah-no not afraid of squaw-brave."

Ha-ha-pah-no had a tongue and a reputation for it, and the Big Tongue did not threaten her any more. Too many squaws and girls joined in the laugh against him. Perhaps the fact that Ha-ha-pah-no had a husband over six feet high had something to do with it, and that Na-tee-kah was the only daughter of Long Bear. It was not safe to quarrel overmuch with either of them. They were almost as safe as a large dog is if he is known to be quick-tempered. Nobody kicks him.

There was an attempt made at pretty fast travelling, for all the wise warriors knew that the tramp across the mountains must be a hard one, however good the trail might be, and there were a good many very sober faces among them. They had lost their horses and their dogs, and now they were leaving behind them a great many other things, and they felt as if hard times had come. Starvation is a very severe school-master.

So, for that matter, is thirst, even if provisions are plentiful, and Sile Parks learned a great lesson of endurance that day. His father had not uttered a word of complaint. Yellow Pine had not murmured, and when Sile said tohim,

"All the men seem to stand it the very best kind," he had all but contemptuously replied,

"Them? Why, every soul on 'em's an old mountain man. Not a greenhorn or a tenderfoot among 'em. You won't catch one on 'em a whimperin', not if they die for it."

So there were other men besides red Indians who were able to suffer and be silent, and Sile tried hard to be that kind of man; but long before sunset he felt as if he were choking.

The mountains to the westward loomed up larger and less cloudily as the worn-out teams were urged forward. The trail pointed steadily towards them, and Yellow Pine unhesitatingly asserted that they were on the righttrack.

"No mistake about it, jedge. It ain't no common cross-prairie trail. It's one of their old migration tracks. They've been a treadin' of it sence the year one."

The "year one" was a good while ago, but a good deal of hard tramping, by many bisons, year after year, had been required to make that ancient cattle-path. No grass had grown upon it for nobody could guess how many generations, and it was likely to be in the way of ploughing whenever that plain should be turned into farming-land.

The greatest care was taken of the animals, those in the traces being taken out and changed frequently, and at last all the riders dismounted and led their horses. Yellow Pine every now and then went around and examined to see how things were looking, and Sile went with him.

"They'll stan' it, every critter of 'em," he said, repeatedly. "They're all good stock; good condition. I picked 'em out."

"Your mare is the ugliest in the lot," said Sile, recklessly.

"Best though. Out-walk, out-run, and out-starve any critter in the outfit, 'cepting me."

"Can you out-travel a horse?"

"Course I can—most horses. I don't know 'bout the old mare. She can out-travel anything. She's good tempered, too; knows just when it's the right time to kick and break things. Oh but can't she tear, though!"

He looked at her affectionately, as if her very temper were one of her virtues, and she glanced back at him, showing the whites of her eyes in a way that indicated anything but a placid mind.

"She's always riley when she doesn't get plenty to drink," said Pine, "but she hasn't kicked once in all this. Knows it isn't any fault of mine. We'll git there, old lady. Don't you go off the handle."

Another hour and the mountains were very tall, and looked cool, and seemed to promise all sorts of things.

"The mines we are after are in among 'em," said Judge Parks to his son.

"Our trip across the plains has been a quick one; all the quicker for this push."

"Hope there'll be a good spring of water right in the edge of them," said Sile, but his voice was huskier than ever and he was struggling against a feeling of faintness.

"Poor fellow!" said the judge to himself. "I mustn't say too much to him. It's an awful time for me."

So it was, for every now and then the thought would come to him,

"What if, after all, we should not find water when we get there?"

The sun sank lower and lower, and now at last Yellow Pine stood still and leaned against his mare, pointing forward.

"Jedge! Jedge—there they are!"

"What is it, Pine?"

The judge could hardly speak, and Sile had such a ringing in his ears that he could hardly hear, but Yellow Pine gasped out,

"Them there mesquite scrubs. I was just a beginning to say to myself, what if I'd mistook the lay of the land, and there they are. I went through 'em last spring was a year ago. It's all right!"

The men tried hard to cheer, but it was of no manner of use. All they could do was to plod on and drag their horses after them. The teams in the wagons halted again and again, panting and laboring, and every slight roll of the plain was a tremendous obstacle, but all was overcome, inch by inch.

Yellow Pine had evidently felt his responsibility as guide more deeply than he had been willing to confess. He led on now with his mouth open and panting, for he had given his own last ration of water to Sile Parks and was thirstier than the rest of them. So, for that matter, had Sile's father, but some men suffer more from thirst than others and the judge had held out remarkably. Just inside the range of mesquites Yellow Pine stopped short.

"Bufler been killed here inside of two days," he exclaimed. "Must be Indians nigh, somewhere. Keep an eye out, boys."

It was no time for any caution that included delay, and he walked on like a man who knew exactly where he was, and all followed him, the men cutting away the bushes here and there to let the wagons pass more easily. On, on, until at last Yellow Pine reached the spring.

"Here it is," he said faintly, and then he lay down by it and began to drink slowly, using his hand for a cup.

"Boys," said Judge Parks, "be careful how you drink too much at first. Take it easy. Sponge the mouths of the horses and then let them have a little at a time. Sile, my poor boy, come with me."

Sile was making a tremendous effort. He had been doing it all day. He almost wanted to cry when he saw that spring of water. Then he wanted to laugh, but his mouth was too dry for that. All he could do was to smile in a sickly sort of way and take the cup his father held out to him. There was only a little water in the bottom of it.

"Oh father, give me some more."

"Not yet, Sile. Sit right down and wait till you get the effect of that. Hold it in your mouth before you swallow it. I don't mean to let you kill yourself."

"Aha! But isn't it good? There isn't anything else quite so good as water."

"That's a fact, Sile, but it's like a great many other good things, you don't know the value of it until you've had to go without it."

A full hour was spent in getting men and animals ready to drink without injury, and Yellow Pine at last declared, triumphantly,

"Jedge, we've won the riffle; we won't lose a hoof. All the men are doing first-rate too. This 'ere's my old campin'-ground, but there's been an Indian camp here since sun-up."

"How do you know that, Pine?"

"Found live fire. There hasn't been any dew on it to put it out. What's more, they've gone on into the mountains. Hunting-party. We're all right, jedge."

The mining expedition now kindled fires of its own, and something was done in the way of getting supper. There was no grass, but the horses and mules could attend fairly well to the contents of their nose-bags, and the men paid them all manner of attention. Only a greenhorn is careless of the comfort and welfare of his horse.

Sile drank well at last, under his father's direction, and then he felt like eating something. After that it seemed to him as if the whole world had only been made as a good place to sleep in. He did not care whether the tents were pitched or not. All he wanted was a piece of ground large enough to lie on, and a blanket, and he was ready to sleep as soundly and silently as if he had been one of the mountains which raised their shadowy heads into the light of the rising moon. He had been without water for the first time in his life. He had stood it through heroically, he had found a spring, and now he needed a long sleep.

Chapter IX

INTO A NEW WORLD

Two Arrows wiped the blood of the cougar from the blade of his lance. He was glad it was a good lance. His father had traded a pony for it, as he well knew, with a Mexican, years before that, and it was no ordinary weapon. He had chosen it from among half a dozen, as the very thing with which to do something uncommon, and now it had proved its value. He almost felt an affection for that lance.

One-eye had lain down close to the dead body of the cougar, as if watching him for any returning signs of life. If that great cat had quivered, there was a dog ready to shake the quiver out of him.

"It's all good meat," said Two Arrows, "but what shall I do with it?"

There was but one answer to that question. He took off the skins of both animals, cut them up as well as he could, carried all the meat he did not need at once to a cool place among the rocks, piled stones over it and left it. He had no ice-house, and that was the best he could do, but he made a fire and ate plentifully of antelope venison, and of what the Western men call "painter meat." It was hard for him to say which he liked the best. Then he took a bit of charcoal and made his mark upon the rocks where he buried his game. He was immensely proud of his right to do that. He scored two very large and distinct arrows, heaped on some more heavy stones, shouted to One-eye, and again pushed forward. His exploring trip was already brimming full of glory and adventure, and he was ready to fight all the cougars in the mountains. So was One-eye, for he had had one of the biggest dinners he had ever eaten, and not another dog on hand to dispute it with him. He seemed to be possessed with an idea that that place must have more antelopes and mountain-cats in it, and that he was likely to find some of them behind rocks. He was doubtless right on the main point, but not a stone of the many he smelled under turned him out a cougar or a big-horn. Hunting was over for that day, and so much time had been consumed that Two Arrows felt like running to make it up. He did but walk, however, and as the road was now all the way downhill, like a bad man's life, he walked easily. The great gorge widened until its broken walls stretched away to the right and left, and the eager-hearted explorer came out from among the scattered rocks at a point from which he could suddenly see a great deal. Away beyond and below him spread such a scene as he could hardly have hoped for, and yet which can be found in hundreds of places all over the mountain country of the American continent. Just such scenes are to be found among the Alps, the Andes, the Himalayas, and every other similar group of rocky upheavals, but Two Arrows knew of no other country than his own, the one his band of Nez Percés had hunted and feasted and starved in.

It was a great, deep, grassy, well-wooded, well-watered valley, the very home of game and a sure promise of all comfort to a hunter. How far it might reach to the westward no eye could tell, for the prospect was bounded by other mountains, and there were plain tokens that a considerable stream ran through the middle of it.

"Much water, perhaps," said Two Arrows. "Must go somewhere. Find out some day."

The idea of a river suggested the other idea that it could be followed until an ambitious boy could ascertain where it went to. All that was swallowed up at once by the immediate desire to get down upon that green grass and among those trees. One-eye had seen the valley, but was inclined to stick pretty closely at the side of his master. There were only two of them, and they might need each other's help at any moment.

The road tramped by the bison herds did not wind much, as it went on down towards the level ground, but it lazily picked out the easiest slopes and turned the corners of the great rocks on good curves. As Two Arrows and his faithful companion wound around one of these curves, almost at the bottom of the long descent, they suddenly came upon a discovery that startled them. Even the dog pricked up his ears and began to growl, and Two Arrows stepped quickly back behind the rock. He had never been in a white man's village, but he had seen a fort and a few houses around it, and he had seen the houses of Mexican Indians and some others, built of "adobe" or sunburnt brick. He was not, therefore, a judge of such matters, and what he saw filled him with astonishment. He was not exactly alarmed, for a house could not chase him, but he exclaimed,

"Pale-face lodge. Good many. Very bad. What can he do now?"

He peered silently forth for several minutes, but not a human being was in sight. There were no signs of life, no curling smoke, no barking dogs, no cattle, nothing but scattered structures of stone. These must have been put there by somebody, but it began to look as if whoever had built them had gone to some other hunting-ground.

Two Arrows noted everything with eyes that grew more brilliant in their swift and searching glances. There could hardly be any danger in such a solitude as that, but the occasion required caution, and the young "brave" made his advances from cover to cover as if there were eyes in every stone of those houses. One-eye crept at his side with his head and tail up, very much as if there had been game ahead. It was a curious piece of business. The nearer they drew to the objects of their curiosity the safer and lonelier became the appearance of all things. Some of the stone walls had tumbled down, and not one of them had a roof over it of any sort. That was nothing to Two Arrows. For all he knew there were tribes of cunning and wicked pale-faces who built their lodges without roofs. If the world contained anything cunning and wicked and dangerous, in the mind of Two Arrows it was a pale-face. He had been brought up to look upon a white man as a being to be watched, and as an evil to be avoided or destroyed, as the case might be, and yet as a sort of magician, capable of doing wonders, and of bringing the richest presents in all the earth.

He now at last felt confidence and courage to actually crawl through an opening of one of those walls and look around him. It was one great, empty room, strewn with bits of stone, and growing thickly, here and there, were grass and tall weeds.

"Nobody here for ever so long," had already been his conclusion, and he was thoroughly satisfied of it now. He arose and walked around and looked at things in that and every other house. Some of them had windows so high up as to prove that they must have had two or even three stories in some old time when people used them, but those were "signs" that Two Arrows could not read. The main thing to him was that he was still all alone and in perfect safety. If the wisest white man in the world had been there with him, he could not have formed an idea by whom those houses were constructed. Just such ruins have been found in many places among the valleys of the western mountains, and all that learned people can yet do is to guess how they came to be there. The houses did not come up like so many mushrooms, and beyond that they have almost nothing to say for themselves. Two Arrows had no further questions to ask, and One-eye had searched nooks and corners with an assiduity which had been duly rewarded: he had captured a fine, fat rabbit, and he brought it to his master as a sort of token. No rabbit would have made a home in a place infested by white men, for rabbits have the same idea of them that Indians have and for somewhat similar reasons. The rabbits get very little good from them, however, and the Indians a great deal—that is, unless the rabbits live near a white man's farm and garden. In that case they come up fully to the Indian standard and help themselves to all they can get hold of.

Two Arrows picked up the rabbit and walked out to what had been the door of that house. It was nearly sunset, and there could be no more exploring done that day. He looked away off into the valley and saw another token that he was alone in that part of it: no less than three gangs of deer were feeding quietly between him and a bit of forest not more than half a mile away.

Right past the group of old ruins ran a dancing brook of cool, pure water from the mountains, and a better place to camp in could not have been imagined. It was evidently safe to build a fire and cook the rabbit, but for more perfect safety Two Arrows made his blaze on a spot where some old walls prevented the light of it from being seen at too great a distance. After his supper was eaten there came over him a feeling that he had seen and done altogether too much for one boy in one day. He had come out into a sort of new world through a cleft in the mountains, and he did not know that precisely the same thing happens to every boy in the world who makes up his mind to be something. The boys who are contented not to be anything do not have much of a world to live in, anyhow, poor fellows; they only hang around and eat and wear clothes.

Chapter X

SILE'S POCKET

Na-tee-kah had all the load a girl of her size could comfortably carry when she set out with her people. So had all the rest except the dignified warriors. For that reason all the urging in the world could not get out of that dispirited cavalcade one-half the speed attained by Two Arrows and One-eye the previous evening. Na-tee-kah thought continually of her pony, between thoughts of her daring brother and wonderings of what he had done and seen. She knew very well that there is nothing so disables a "plains Indian" as to dismount him. It is not so bad as to break both his legs, but he is so accustomed, from childhood, to use a horse's legs instead of his own that he is like a man lost when he is set on foot. He has learned to hunt on horseback mostly, and all his fighting has been done in the saddle. The old-time Indians of the East and of Cooper's novels had hardly any horses, and in their deep forests could not have used them to advantage. What the far Western tribes did in those days nobody knows, but all the tribes which have migrated out of the woods into the prairie country have become "pony-men."

Na-tee-kah could not remember another time when she, daughter of a chief, had been compelled to carry so much, even for a short distance. She knew how to pack a pony capitally well, for that is one of the first arts of Nez Percé house-keeping. When and where should they ever get some more ponies? Her father was a renowned horse-thief, and so were several others of the best warriors in the band, and there was hope in that thought; still there is a double difficulty before a man who sets out to steal horses without having one of his own to ride.

"Two Arrows will steal horses some day," she said to Ha-ha-pah-no, confidently.

"Big chief: steal a heap. No boy any more. Big Tongue find a horse; say he stole him. No brave. Pony come somehow."

Nobody else in that band could have guessed how the mind of Long Bear himself was busy with plans concerning that very matter. He thought of all the horses of all the tribes at any kind of difference with the Nez Percés, and he thought of the white traders and their rich droves of quadrupeds of all sorts. He had won his rank fairly, as his son was likely to do after him, and he had a great deal of courage and ambition; just at present, however, he was a dismounted horse-thief, and he felt the disgrace of it even more than the inconvenience. It was a sad thing to be afoot at his time of life, and he brooded over it like some great white merchant who had suddenly failed in business. He feared that it would take some time to set up that band again, without any four-footed capital to begin on.

It was pleasant to find the trail so good, at all events, and before dark they made out to reach the very spot where Two Arrows had camped. They had been more than twice as long in getting there, but the first brave who pushed on into the open space found the dead embers of a fire and began to study them. Not far behind him were Na-tee-kah and Ha-ha-pah-no, and it was hard to say which of them was the first to point at the black coals and ashes, and exclaim, "Two Arrows!"

The word was echoed from lip to lip until it came to Long Bear and his wife. For a wonder he was walking beside her, which was as near as he could come to carrying her load for her. She was only the step-mother of Na-tee-kah and her brother, and had a pappoose of her own as part of her burden, but she took her full share of the family pride when her husband drew himself grimly up and shut off the strong temptation to "whoop."

"Young brave," he said to her with great calmness. "Great chief some day. All like father. Same. Go steal pony pretty soon."

The camp was quickly made, and there was food for all in moderate allowance. They were certain of resting in perfect security, and in the morning they were as eager as Two Arrows had been to push on out of such narrow quarters. Nothing happened to any of them until late in the day, and then the whole band went suddenly into camp again.

The Big Tongue had become almost a silent Indian under the effects of hard walking, but he had been stung again by remarks from Ha-ha-pah-no, and he had gone ahead. He had not gone far enough to make him look enterprising, but all at once the cañon fairly rang with a whoop he sent back, to let the rest know he had found something. At the same moment three great vultures, or buzzard-eagles, arose from a prize they had found, and soared away. They were wonderfully wide-winged birds, and each carried off a good dinner, for they had nearly finished the offal left upon the ground by the carcasses of the cougar and the big-horn.

The Big Tongue pointed proudly at the discovery he had made, and was about to say something, when he was once more overwhelmed. His whooping had brought a swarm of the braves around him, but of course no squaws had presumed to push in. It was for that very cause that the eyes of Na-tee-kah had been busy among the rocks, and so she had discovered the charcoal "token" scored upon one of them.

"Two Arrows!" she screamed, and in a moment more there were warriors there, taking away the stones which covered the meat and the skins.

It was time now for Long Bear to do all the whooping there was in him. His son had slain a cougar single-handed, and had killed a big-horn, and here were the proofs of it. The whole band could at once have another feast of fresh meat, provided by the young hero, for whom they were indebted to the great Long Bear.

It was decided that they had travelled far enough for one day, but that an early start should be made the next morning. That had also been an interesting day at the camp by the spring.

The over-wearied pale-faces slept well, but Yellow Pine arose three times to go around among the animals and see how they were doing. He had them all fed and rubbed down most carefully in the morning. It was a good thing to do, and when Sile Parks awoke and stretched himself, he felt as if he also wanted to be fed and rubbed down. Almost everybody else was already astir, and breakfast was soon ready for him.

Yellow Pine did a deal of exploring, before and after he breakfasted, and Sile at once set out to imitate him. He asked some question or other of every one he saw, and believed that he had learned a great deal. At last he came to a heap of stones and bushes that seemed to him to have been piled up remarkably.

"How could they ever have got there?" he said, as he began to pull upon a bush with green leaves yet clinging to its twigs. In five minutes more he knew where the Nez Percés had made their hasty "cache" for their lodges and other treasures, and he went at once to report it to his father and to Yellow Pine. The latter looked at Sile with positive respect, and exclaimed,

"There now, jedge; that settles it. I know I'm right; them Indians had lost their ponies. I couldn't find a hoof-mark on their trail this morning; they dragged some lodge-poles along, though. I say, we must leave their cache jest as we found it. We must foller right along, too, or we'll run short of fodder. They've taken my old road. We needn't be afraid of 'em, only we'd best keep a sharp lookout."

Horses and mules and all felt as if a day's rest would be as good as a treat; but after all was said and done it was decided to keep moving. The start made was not an early one, and there was work for all hands here and there. The herds of bisons had not prepared that road for the passage of wagon wheels, and it needed the axe in one place and the crow-bar in another before the teams could pass. There was no sort of danger that the Nez Percés would be caught up with by the mining-party, and Yellow Pine seemed to breathe more freely at the end of every mile.

"No, jedge," he said; "we won't have to leave the outfit anywhere. There'll be a heap of hard work at some spots, but we can make our way through, and we can come and go by this track forever after it's well opened."

Sile Parks learned a great deal that day about the mysteries of road-making; he also learned how much a really well-built wagon will stand if it is not too heavily loaded. For all that, however, the best part of his time was expended in staring at the peaks, and in searching the walls of the cañon for traces of gold and silver ore.

"Father," said he at last, at a place where the wagons were "stuck" for a while, "I'm going ahead to see what'll turn up."

"Don't go too far, that's all."

"Keep yer eye out for mines," shouted Yellow Pine, with a laugh, and Sile took it seriously.

"It's a gold country," he said to himself, "and I might stumble upon some of it."

That was precisely what he made out to do. He was marching along, with his eyes on all the rocky precipices, as if the mouth of a gold-mine might open to him at any moment, and he was not so careful of his feet as he should have been. A loose stone shot away from under him, and down he came upon a fairly level floor of sand and gravel. It was so sudden and so sharp a dropping that he sat still for a moment and looked around him.

"Halloo, what's that?" Something bright and yellow had caught his eye, peering out at him from the gravel his boot-heel had disturbed. "Gold! gold! A chunk of gold!"

Thousands upon thousands of "placer miners" have raised precisely such a shout in just such sandy gullies, but Sile felt as if he were the first being on earth to whom such an experience had ever happened. He at once began to dig and sift among the gravel fiercely. He took out his hunting-knife and plied it as a trowel. Little bits of dull yellow metal rewarded him every now and then until he worked along to where a ledge (or the edge of one) of quartz came nearly to the surface. On the upper side of that, and lying closely against it, he pried out something that made him shout "Hurrah!" and that then gave him almost a sick feeling. It was a gathering of golden nuggets and particles which would nearly have filled his hat, and there were others like it, only smaller, all along the edge of that stone. For unknown centuries it had been serving as a "bar" in the natural "washer" made by that ravine, and had caught and kept whatever the torrents had borne down from crumbling quartz rocks above and had drifted against it.

Sile thought of Aladdin and his wonderful lamp; then he thought of the California miners; then he shut his eyes for a moment. Then he went on digging, and hc was hard at it when a tall form stooped over him and the voice of Yellow Pine exclaimed,

"I'd call it—If the youngster hasn't lighted onto a placer and scooped the biggest kind of a pocket! Sile, you've done it. You can jest ax me all the fool questions you've a mind to after this. You was really learnin' by 'em."

Chapter XI

A TRAPPED BOY

When the light awoke Two Arrows, he found One-eye standing guard as if he did not like the look of things, but no danger showed itself. It was a new country—too much so, perhaps—and a dog with a high sense of duty could not be too careful. Two Arrows also had duties, and he felt that one of them was to go back at once and tell his band what he had discovered. He had no idea that they were already on the march, or he might have been less troubled in mind about them. His other duty, not quite so plain, was to explore the valley a little and see how many buffaloes and deer and all that sort of thing were in it. He wondered at the greenness of the grass, not knowing that the mountain range east of it took care of that, taking the water out of the winds from the west so that they were often sponge-dry when they passed over upon the parching plains beyond. He had never heard of Eden and he could not make any comparisons, but he roundly declared that he had never been in a place that promised better hunting. He did not even ask himself how a herd of bisons should remember what their fathers had told them about that valley and come hundreds of miles to find grass there. He had not seen one yet, but he had caught a glimpse of a gang of deer in rapid motion. That fact set him to thinking and made him cautious, for it was an hour when deer are feeding unless they have been disturbed. He cooked and ate his breakfast, providing liberally for One-eye, but could hardly make up his mind in which direction to go. There was the mouth of the cañon, telling him one thing, and in all other directions were the possible secrets of that valley.

His feet took him along, at last, and he wandered for nearly a mile before he came to any sort of adventure. Then he suddenly discovered why the deer were in motion, and why it was time for him and One-eye to wander back again. It was almost as bad as a war-party of another tribe or even a band of wicked pale-faces, for at the edge of a little grove of wild plum-trees One-eye broke out into something between a howl and a bark, and turned, running towards his master. Then Two Arrows himself turned and ran, for his quick eyes caught the meaning of it. The head of a grisly bear came out between two bushes, and no idea of heroism called for any waiting. The cañon, or the ruins, or almost any other place, would have been better, at that moment, than the spot where he was when Bruin saw him.

The grisly may have had bad-luck that morning. At all events, he was out after game, and was in a bad temper. He hated all dogs, naturally, and he had seen One-eye. He hated men, as well, but his first rush was after the scared quadruped. That was an excellent thing for Two Arrows. He was the best runner of his age in his band, and never before had he done quite so well, but he stuck to his weapons. His bag of provisions had been hidden among the old houses, and he was glad of it as he bounded away across the grass. Every jump counted, for One-eye was doing the right thing. He was not following his master too closely, he was only thinking of getting away from that bear. He, too, had been the best runner of his tribe, when there had been other dogs to run with him, and he certainly was now. He ran well, but so did the bear, for a good horse does not too easily overtake a grisly, and a man on foot can never do it if the bear does his best.

It was an exciting race, but Two Arrows knew it must have an end some time. He longed for a tree, and to be away up in the top of it, but there were none near enough to be of any use. He kept an eye on the other racers, and it was not many minutes before he saw that One-eye was doing almost too well. He was getting away so fast that the grisly gave him up and turned to his other chance for a breakfast. It was as if he had said to himself,

"Dogs are no good. They run too well. A nice, tender, well-fed Indian boy, now, and I'll get him in a moment."

Two Arrows had gained a pretty good start, and it led him towards the cañon. He tried to calculate the distance, and how long it would take him to get there, but his next thought was that he had never heard of a grisly that could gallop and rush like this one.

"It'll all be over with me. I'd fight him, but he's too much for me. Got to die now."

It was an awful moment, and all the courage in him did not make it any less so. The claws and jaws and hug of a mountain grisly are a terrible prospect to set before anybody's ambition.

Just then another prospect and a ray of hope dawned upon him. Away to the right he saw a solitary bowlder of gray granite, with a round top, nearly thirty feet above the grass.

"If it isn't too smooth to climb," flashed through the mind of Two Arrows, as he turned and ran for it. He was running now for his life, and the bear was rapidly gaining on him, but it told well for his valor that he did not drop lance or bow.

Nearer, now, and he could see that the rock was one of those bald-headed, smooth-cheeked affairs that look as if they had been ground and polished in a mill.

"Ugh! Other side, maybe," groaned Two Arrows, as he dodged around the hopeless side he came to. Away around, and the same mocking smoothness made his heart sink, while the fierce growl of the huge wild beast behind him thrilled him through and through.

"Ugh! rough place! Climb."

It was a mere crack at the surface of the ground, but at a few feet above it the granite surface was somewhat broken. A good spring, aided by the tough shaft of his lance, and Two Arrows managed to brace himself upon a tolerable holding. If he should slip there would be an end of it, for the grisly was close up now. He clung like a fly, and found place after place for his hands and feet. In a moment more he was sitting upon the round top of the rock safe, but a prisoner, with a guard set to keep him secure. He had come out after adventures and he had found one of the very largest kind. He had never heard such tremendous roaring growls as the disappointed grisly was now uttering. Between these he could also hear, at no great distance, the mournful howls of One-eye. The sagacious animal had not self-conceit enough to match his weight and size against a brute that could have whipped a lion in five minutes, but he could express his feelings concerning the state of affairs.

"He can't get up here," said Two Arrows, but he said it doubtfully, for the grisly is a rock bear, and is made for climbing. He was now studying the face of that rock at the cleft, and it was not long before he made up his mind that he could do something.

"I won't waste any arrows on him," said the boy on the top of the bowlder. "Besides, if I don't get him too angry he may go off."

Not without trying a climb for his human game; and it was wonderful with what care and consideration, as well as skill and strength, Bruin made his effort.

Two-Arrows lay down, bow in hand, and watched him, as he raised his huge bulk against the side of the rock. The long, strong, cruel-looking claws took hold of crevices and roughnesses much more powerfully than a human hand or foot could have grasped them. A grunt, a growl, a great lift, and the grisly was off the ground.

"He is coming. Let him come one length nearer."

Two Arrows did not know that he was testing his quality as a warrior and chief to be. It was a marvellous trial of cool courage to lie there, with an arrow on the string, and bide his time.

"Now! Ugh!"

The arrow went truly to its mark, but the hide of a grisly is a tough shield, and the shaft did not go as deeply as it might have gone into a deer or bison. Arrow after arrow sped in swift, unerring succession, and the bear received them with roars of fury, struggling upward as his wrath and pain aroused him to greater efforts.

"My last two arrows. One for that leg, just above the claw."

Cool and correct again, and the last brace of shafts did their work to admiration. They did not kill the grisly nor even loosen the gripe of that great forearm and claw upon the rock, but the next struggle of the bear brought him upon smooth stone, gently rounding. He reached out over it with his wounded limb, and the black hooks at the end of it did not work well. His game was within a length of him, but it was game that held a long Mexican lance in its ready hand. Under other circumstances Bruin could have parried that thrust and closed with its giver, but not now. It went through his other forearm, and his gripe with that loosened for a second or so—only for an instant, but that was enough. Slip, slide, growl, tear, roar, and the immense monster rolled heavily to the ground below, full of rage and arrow-wounds, and altogether unfitted for another steep climb.

Two Arrows drew a great breath of relief, but he well knew that he had not yet escaped. There were oceans of hate and fight in the wounded grisly, and there was no use whatever in going down for a fair match with him upon the grass. He was in his most dangerous state, and the top of the rock would have to answer all purposes for a season. There was no telling how long that would be, for even when the bear arose and limped all the way around the bowlder, his ferocious growls plainly declared his purpose. He had not the least idea of letting the matter stop there. He meant to stay and watch it out. Perhaps more grislies would come to help him and keep guard while he should doctor himself. It was a most remarkable trap for a young explorer to get caught in, and he well knew that a grisly will take more killing and die longer and harder than any other known animal. Besides, he had no idea how much or how seriously his shafts had touched the vitals of his enemy.

He must stay where he was, and now he felt something like a sensation of mortification. One-eye had deserted him. All the howling had died away while the bear was climbing the rock. The last dog of that band of Nez Percés had turned tail and left his master on the top of a bowlder to be starved out by a bear.

Chapter XII

THE ERRAND OF ONE-EYE

The wagons came slowly on down the pass, but it was only a few moments before everybody but the two drivers had dismounted and stood gazing at Sile's remarkable "find." There were old "placer miners" among them, and they all declared that it was just the place in which they would have expected a "bonanza." Then they all added that without water to wash the sand and gravel with, there would be little use in doing anything more than to hunt for "pockets." There might be "pay dirt" in all directions, but a man might scratch and sift until he starved and not get more than enough to buy him a new hat. They had been through all that sort of experience, and their heads were not to be turned by it. Still, it was decided to try that level again some day, and the whole cañon, at a time of the year when water was to be had. All that could now be done was to carefully search for and gather up the odds and ends of Sile's "luck." Even the necessity of grass for the horses compelled the train to move onward.

When they came to the rocky ledge, with the precipice on one side and the mountain wall on the other, Judge Parks turned to Yellow Pine with a face full of doubt.

"Don't you be skeered, jedge. I took a measure of it at the narrerest p'int, and it'll let the wheels go by and two feet to spare."

That was close work, when they came to it, and Sile shuddered all over as he saw how near the wheels came to the edge of destruction. A restive mule, a scared horse, a little backing and plunging, and disaster was ready to come. Not an animal shied, however, though some of them trembled and sheered in towards the rock. It was hardest when they had to hold back going down and around some of the sharper curves. Sile had several tremendous shudders at such places and drew long breaths of relief afterwards, as the wagons rolled on in safety. Then, on the next level below, there was more axe and crow-bar work to be done, and it was late in the day when the train once more reached a deserted camping-ground of the band of Indians they seemed to be pursuing.

"We'd better take a rest here, jedge. It's been a hard day on the men and the hosses, and we've struck gold a'ready."

Sile had been strangely aware of that fact for some hours, and it had dazed him a little. He had walked on without asking a question of anybody. He had a dim idea that the metal he had found was worth a great deal of money, but he hardly cared to know how much. It was a new and wonderful sensation. His father told him there was enough of it to buy him a farm and stock it, and when Yellow Pine had finished his other duties, at going into camp, and had noted all the signs the Nez Percés left behind, he said to Sile,

"Now, my boy, gather up all the charcoal you can rake from those dead fires and I'll show you something. Slugs are safer to carry than dust and nuggets. I allers used to slug my finds, first thing."

That was Greek to Sile, but Yellow Pine rummaged one of the wagons and brought out a long-nosed bellows and a crucible and a sort of mould that opened with two handles. He put the crucible in among the coals, filled it from Sile's yellow heap, covered it, and began to work the bellows. Sile was astonished to find how speedily what Pine called "bullion" would melt, and how easy it was to run it into little bars. There did not seem to be so much of it, but there was less danger that any of the smaller chunks and scales and particles could get away.

"There, Sile. There's your farm, cows, hosses, hogs and all, and it only cost you a gitten' thirsty."

"They're wonderful," was all Sile could make out to say, and his father put them in a bag and locked them up in an iron-bound box in one of the wagons.

"You needn't scratch into all the sand you come to after this," said Yellow Pine. "That's what takes the tuck out of placer miners. One good pocket'll most ginerally spile the eyes of a green hand."

He assured the judge that one more push would bring them to good grass, and he added,

"What's more, we ain't in any hurry to ketch up with no redskins till we know what they are. It's peace with most on 'em, but this 'ere isn't a strong band, and I kinder want to feel my way."

There was sense in that, especially as he knew that Indians without horses are also Indians on the lookout for some. What he did not know was the state of mind that band of Nez Percés was in at that hour.

They had set out very early that morning, and were plodding on steadily down the winding slopes of the cañon, when there came to them an unexpected sensation. It was a dog.

Right up the trail trotted One-eye, all alone, and with an air of business anxiety. He neither paused nor turned until he came to Long Bear himself, and in front of the chief he sat down, threw up his head, and let out the most mournful howl he knew—and he knew a great many.

"Where Two Arrows?" asked the chief, as if the dog had been human, and he was answered first by another howl and then by an eager look and a tug at his deer-skin leggings. Then One-eye trotted off a little distance along the trail and looked back and barked, and the dullest man in the world could have understood him. It all plainly meant,

"Come on. There's a fellow down this way that's in need of help. Follow me and help him."

"Ugh!" exclaimed Long Bear, and he added the names of half a dozen of the leading braves. "Two Arrows send dog after warrior. Come."

That was somewhat more than the truth, seeing that all the credit belonged to One-eye, but in a minute or so the old chief was leading his men rapidly down the pass. There was nothing whatever to be said, and One-eye kept well ahead of them, every now and then trying to express an idea he had that no time was to be wasted.

"Ugh!" was all the remark made by any brave when the valley came in sight, and hardly more was remarked upon the ruins of the ancient village, but every grunt meant a great deal.

"Not here. Dog go right on," said Long Bear. "Follow. Find Two Arrows somewhere."

They had not far to go now before they halted as if with one accord. From the summit of a granite bowlder, a hundred yards in advance of them, came a shrill whoop, and there stood the object of their search, firmly erect and seemingly unharmed.

"Boy all right," said Big Tongue. "Better come down."

"Two Arrows no fool," said Long Bear. "Go slow. Watch dog."

One-eye still trotted on, but more slowly, until he turned the corner of the rock. He reappeared in a second, with a sharp, warning yelp, followed by the fierce growling charge of an uncommonly large grisly bear.

"Ugh!" said Long Bear. "Stand still. Boy been treed."

He had not been "treed," he had been bowldered, and the grisly had been arrowed and lanced thoroughly. His angry charge had been made with his last energies, and before he advanced half-way he reeled and fell.

There was no boy upon the rock now. Two Arrows darted down from his perch, slipping, sliding the instant the bear followed One-eye. He had waited up there for hour after hour, looking down at his half disabled enemy, and he was tired of it. He had seen that the strength of the bear was failing and that he bled freely, and was not far behind him when he fell.

"Whoop! whoop! whoop! I have killed a grisly. My bear!" he shouted, and it was all in vain that the Big Tongue ran faster than even the Long Bear himself, for Two Arrows had the advantage of them. His lance was the first to be plunged into the dying monster, and the great brute tore up the sod around him for only half a minute before he stretched himself out and all was over. With the help of several hours of quiet bleeding, which cannot always be provided for in such cases, Two Arrows had fought and killed a grisly single-handed, and again Long Bear was the proudest man in the whole Nez Percé nation. The steepness of the rock had helped a good deal, and the bear had hardly had a fair chance, but after all he had been whipped by a boy of fifteen. It was a disgrace to the grisly but it was a great honor to the young hero, for by all Indian law he was thenceforth entitled to wear the claws of that bear on state occasions. Adding all things together, bisons and big-horn and cougar and grisly, Two Arrows was rapidly getting to be a middle-aged warrior, and the other boys had no hope of catching up with him. He might also fairly be said to have led his band into that valley, and now the pity of it was that they had no ponies to eat such excellent grass.

The remainder of the band came down the pass remarkably, with Na-tee-kah well in advance of everybody else.

"Could anything terrible have happened to Two Arrows?"

Her heart beat hard with exertion and anxiety, and when she reached the level she hurried right along upon the trail of the braves. It was not many minutes before she could see them, and a sort of mist came before her eyes. They were all sitting upon the grass around something, and she could hear her father's voice chanting. It was a curious kind of song of triumph, belonging especially to a case of large grisly bear slaying, but Na-tee-kah could not hear it clearly at first, and it might have been a funeral song for all the music there was in it. All out of breath she toiled on, as near as an Indian girl might come to a party of warriors, and then she understood it like a flash. Red or white, she was only a girl, and she sat down on the grass and began to cry. The Big Tongue had risen as she came near, and he was polite enough to say to her,

"Squaw not cry. Boy all right. We have killed a bear. Ugh!"

Chapter XIII
GREAT SCOUTING

The quadrupeds of the mining expedition showed many signs of the hard time they had been having, and it was needful to get out from among the rocks quickly. It was yet quite shadowy in the deep cañon when the wagons were set in motion, but not a great deal of "road mending" was called for from that point onward. Early in the day they came out upon the level, and before noon the horses and mules were picking the rich grass around the ancient ruins.

It was a grand time, and Sile had a dim idea that he only drew his breath now and then, the great, long ones came so frequently. He had felt one kind of awe in the cañon and in looking at the mountain peaks. Now he felt quite another kind of awe in looking at the rude mason-work of those houses.

"Father," he asked, "do you s'pose they were people anything like us?"

"They built three-story houses. No Indians ever did that."

"Is there nothing at all about them in history?"

"Yes, here are the ruins. Here are little books like this."

He handed Sile what looked for all the world like a broken piece of an old pot, and Sile said so.

"That's it. If it is one, it shows that they understood making pottery. Nobody has ever found anything to prove that they were miners, and all the stones of these houses are only broken. None of them are cut or trimmed."

It was a wonder of wonders to stand there and talk about a lost and vanished people, but Yellow Pine was thinking of a people who had vanished without being lost. They were the Indians whose camp-grounds he had moved into and out of, and he had an idea that they might be found again at any hour. He advised the judge not to move on again until some exploring and scouting should have been done. Meantime the "critters," as he called them, did their feeding under a strong guard and close watching.

"Sile," he said, "as soon as your horse has had a good feed, you and I will ride a circuit and see what we can find."

Sile's blood danced a little. Scouting after Indians was a thing he had read about, and he did not dwell too much upon the fact that he was chosen to go with Pine rather because his horse was a fast one and had not pulled wagons than for any reason. Pine said to him,

"Your eyes are pretty good ones, too. Who knows but what you might see something. Jedge, I won't run him into any danger. Them Indians is all on foot."

Sile set to work at once upon his repeating-rifle, his revolver, and the edge of his hunting-knife, as if he had a battle with Pawnees on hand. He gave up studying the ruins at once, and even forgot how many nuggets his gold had been run into. He had never before felt precisely that kind of excitement, and was too young to know that every entirely new enthusiasm is worth a whole book in the way of education, if it comes rightly. People who have never been waked up are apt to be dull people.

It was an old story to Yellow Pine, and when at last they both were mounted and ready to ride away, it was worth while to look at his cast-iron face and then at that of Sile Parks.

"Sile," said his father, as he looked at him, "bring me in some Indians; not a whole tribe; just a few."

"Come on, Sile," said Pine. "We'll bring all we find, I reckon."

He showed no disposition to ride fast, but cantered away to the right, skirting the edge of the mountain slope, and seeming to study every clump of trees and bushes they came to. It was mostly grassy "open" for quite a distance from the mouth of the cañon.

"No smoke anywhere," said Pine. "They're not camped hereaway."

"I walked out along their trail, at the ruins," said Sile. "Why didn't you follow it?"

"That's a fair question, Sile. It looks as if I'd orter ha' done it, but you see, I don't want to ketch up with 'em or let 'em know we're here. I want to find 'em without telling 'em what road I kem by."

It was a sort of half-Indian cunning, but it was not quite equal to the needs of the matter. Full-blooded Indian cunning beat it all to pieces, as they were to find out before morning. It came to pass in a perfectly easy and natural sort of way.

When the entire band of Nez Percés had arrived, and every soul in it had taken a look at the dead grisly, they had no notion of walking back a single rod. The braves had noted the indications of running water in the distance, and they pushed on until they found a camp-ground on the border of a swift, bright stream, almost alive with trout. It was bordered by a wide band of forest, and the trees were magnificent. Here at last they could all sit down in a kind of peace and plenty, and mourn for their dogs and ponies.

Two Arrows had no mourning to do. What he really needed was to be hooped, like a barrel, for fear his pride and ambition might burst him. He felt as if he were about ten feet high and weighed more than a horse. All the other Indians he had heard of were nothing at all to what he was or was pretty soon going to be. He almost despised cougars and even grislies until he recalled how he had felt when the open jaws of the one which had hunted him came up over the curve of the bowlder.

It occurred to him that he had better have a rock or something to help him next time, but his vanity suggested that after all he had invented that rock. The other Indian boys hardly felt like speaking to him, and Na-tee-kah called him to supper as respectfully as if he had been a full-grown warrior. He felt like one, and as if the camp were too small for him; so he walked out of it after supper, and his feet carried him farther. They seemed to have an idea of their own that it would be good for him to take another look at the bowlder where he had been watched for by the grisly. A thorough understanding of that matter might have taken him down a little, but he was to have better medicine yet before he again reached his father's lodge. He had his bow and arrows with him but no lance, and it was getting too dusky for hunting. The ground he was walking over was pretty level but it had its hollows, and as he came up out of one of these he suddenly dropped flat upon the grass. He had not been hurt, but he had seen something that in a manner knocked him down. It was the biggest surprise he had had since he came through the cañon, for two pale-faces on horseback were cantering along at no great distance. They had not seen him, he was sure of that, although they were evidently looking for something. He let them pass and go on until he felt safe in following. Every nerve in his body tingled with fierce excitement.

"War-path!" he exclaimed. "Ugh! Two Arrows a brave now. Get horse. Big warrior. Grow a heap. Find pale-face camp."

Running, walking, creeping, as the mists of evening deepened, the young Nez Percé followed those two horsemen, cunningly avoiding all detection. He followed them to the edge of the rocky ground at the foot of the mountain slope, and there he saw them turn to the left.

"Know now," he muttered. "Pale-face came through cañon. Follow Nez Percé. Got plenty horse. Two Arrows great brave. Ugh!"

He should have gone for help and have performed the rest of his task in older company, but he was full to over-flowing with the vanity of winning another "heap" of glory. He felt entirely competent to deal with one band of white men, and to carry all their horses into his own camp. His rapid successes had been too much for him, and it is sometimes very nearly the same with young fellows of a different color.

He lost sight of his human game several times, and it was now pretty dark, but his keen eyes caught the glow of camp-fires at last, and he knew what that meant. What he did not know was that Yellow Pine and Sile had ridden a wide circuit across that open and had discovered no sign of danger.

"Them Indians," said Pine, as they were riding in, "have gone on to the timber. They can't have the least idee that we're here, on the ground they passed over. To-morrer we must make another scout, though I sha'n't be easy till I know jest what kind of neighbors we're to have."

That was common-sense, and so was the extreme care with which the quadrupeds were gathered and hobbled and "corralled" between the protecting masses of the ruins. The members of the mining party were already divided into "watches," taking regular turns, and Sile and a man named Jonas were in the first watch with Yellow Pine. That gave him a chance for an unbroken sleep when his work was done. What was also good, it gave him a rest to get sleepy in, and to let all the steam of his excitement get away from his head. He ate well, and he felt somewhat weary afterwards, but there was a queer idea growing in his mind that he was in the neighborhood of strange Indians, and that nobody could tell what might turn up.

"Pine," said he, "if I see an Indian shall I kill him?"

"Yell first, and get out of his way, unless he holds out his hand and says 'How?' But you won't have any chance this night."

Chapter XIV
A WRESTLING MATCH

The moon was to come up late that night, and all the first part of it would be lighted only by stars and camp-fires. The mining party had but two of these latter burning low, and the Nez Percé band had not any, after they had done their cooking, but the stars sent down enough light to make things visible at short distances. The two camps were not over four miles apart.

The only really wide-awake watchman in one of them was One-eye, and he patrolled in all directions as if he had an idea that matters must be less secure in the absence of his wonderful young master. Only one dog to do the barking for a whole village was something very uncommon in Indian history, but it was well to have the great duty given to an entirely competent dog.

The boy whom One-eye considered the greatest personage in all that valley had now crept near enough to the mining camp to get a fair idea of what it contained. He saw a wealth of horse-flesh and mule-flesh, every quadruped of it worth half a dozen Indian ponies, and his ambition almost lifted him up from the grass. It stirred any amount of reckless daring, and it made him remember all the stories he had ever heard of famous chiefs who stole into camps and then stripped them clean of everything. He was already that kind of chief in his own estimation, and did not know that within a hundred yards of him there sat a white boy, of about his own age, not so tall but broader in the shoulders, who was at that moment recalling a long list of just such stories.

Sile had fairly read up on Indian fiction before he left home, and his ideas of the way some things could be done were a little misty. He could hardly sit still for one moment, and preferred to stroll around among the horses to make sure no red man's hand was reaching out for one of them. Old Pine smiled grimly now and then, for he felt perfectly safe on the Indian question, but at last he heard an unaccountable rustling at one end of the corral, and then a loud hurrah from Sile.

The idea had been in Sile's head that his proper course was to go about very much as if he were himself about to steal the horses, and his noiseless movements carried him to the outer edge of the corral at exactly the right moment. He was standing at the side of a tall mule, in the shadow of it and completely hidden, when he saw something darker than a shadow glide out from between two tall weeds and swiftly writhe its way forward. His heart beat like a trip-hammer. His first thought was to use his rifle, but it was a new and dreadful thing to take a human life, and he could not lift his weapon. His eyes said, "Not a large Indian," and his hands let go of the rifle. The next instant, and just as Two Arrows rose to his feet, Sile sprang forward and grappled with him.

It was a most perilous thing to do, considering that Two Arrows carried a knife; but the young Nez Percé had also been thinking, and had made up his mind that "war" was no part of his errand. His tribe was at peace with the pale-faces, except as to horse-flesh, and that fact saved Sile's life. He had been accounted the best wrestler in his set, at home and at school, and his muscles were in capital order. It was not by any means an uneven match, therefore, and Two Arrows would have been glad enough to get away. He had no clothing for Sile to hold him by, and there was more and more danger of losing him every moment, but the shout of warning had hardly begun to rouse the general camp before a pair of long, sinewy arms wound around poor Two Arrows from behind.

"I've got him," said Yellow Pine. "Run for a rope. You're jest the luckiest youngster I ever knowed."

By the time the rope was there, every man in camp was up and out, and the grass and weeds within sight had rifle muzzles pointed at everything among them as big as a human head.

"No whoopin' sounded," said Yellow Pine. "This cub was alone. I say, you young coyote, you jest answer my questions now, or I'll tan the hide clean off ye."

Two Arrows drew himself up proudly and looked at him in silence, but Pine led his captive on into the fire-light and picked up a heavy "black-snake" whip, for he was justly angry.

It was a terrible come-down for the ambition of a young chief. Captured on his first raid and threatened with a horsewhipping. He felt ready to burst, but it was not with vanity this time.

"Where's yer band? Where's their camp?" asked Pine, with a significant flourish of the black-snake, but the Indian boy looked him unflinchingly in the face without a sound or a motion.

"Speak, now," began Pine; but Sile had finished answering some hurried questions from his father, and he now asked one for himself.

"I say, Yellow Pine, didn't I grab him first? Isn't he my prisoner as much as he is yours?"

"What do you mean?"

"Well, now, I don't want him flogged. He didn't use his knife. You always said it was best to be friends with 'em."

"I'd call it— Jcdge, it's jest so. Sile's right. I'd kinder lost my head. Look a-here, redskin, next time you come for hosses you won't get off so easy. I'll unhitch ye now, and let ye up. There now, Sile, shake hands with him."

"How?" said Sile, as he held out his hand to the loosened captive.

"How?" said Two Arrows, and he said it a little sullenly, but he had been glancing from Pine's face to Sile's and understood pretty well that the latter had stopped the proposed work of the black-snake.

"Make him a present of something, Sile," said his father. "Here—give him this."

It was a small round pocket-mirror, worth twenty-five cents, but there was no telling what it was worth in the estimation of such a boy as Two Arrows—perhaps a pound or so of gold nuggets, if he had them, or the skin of his grisly bear, after the glory of killing it had worn a little thin. At all events, he was a most astonished Indian. Evidently these monsters in human form were disposed to be friends with him—particularly this red-headed young chief who had proved himself so good a wrestler. All he had ever heard of pale-faces was against believing it, but there was no chance of escaping from the ring of riflemen now gathered around him, and he gave it up. He answered Yellow Pine's questions by signs only, until something he said brought an exclamation from the old miner Jonas.

"Nez Percé! He's a Nez Percé, Pine. I know their lingo. He can talk some English, too. He needn't play 'possum any longer."

Two Arrows felt that he was completely beaten, and even pride failed to carry him any farther. It came to his mind, also, with a peculiar force, that he was by no means sure of the approval of Long Bear and his warriors. They had not sent him out to kill pale-faces and bring upon them the vengeance of the terrible "brass-button men" he had heard of. He had seen a few of them, and had wondered at their great knives, twice as long as his arm. He decided to speak out now, and in a few moments Jonas had pumped him thoroughly.

"He isn't on any war-path," said Yellow Pine to Judge Parks; "he's jest a fool of a boy. We'll keep him till mornin' and carry him over to his own camp. It's the best way in the world to make friends with 'em."

"All right," replied the judge; "we must get out some presents. See that he doesn't get away."

"I'll look out for that—you bet I will."

So he did, and Two Arrows had now no knife with which to cut the rope whereby he was tied to Yellow Pine's elbow when that "big brave" lay down again. Sile rolled himself up in a blanket, only a few feet from them, and hardly slept a wink. He had captured a wild red Indian
and it beat all the novels he had ever seen.
He did not hear his father chuckle to himself, nor could he read the thoughts of the old judge. Long Bear himself was not prouder of Two Arrows and his grisly than was Sile's father of the manner in which his own boy had met and grappled with a sudden peril.

"He'll be at the head of something or other some day," he muttered, as he was dropping asleep.

Not even Na-tee-kah knew anything of the movements or whereabouts of Two Arrows this time, and her father questioned her in vain. His absence was "irregular," and when the hours went by and he did not return, the Long Bear's face put on an expression of stern displeasure.

"Boy too big," he said; "grow too fast. Brave too soon. Young chief, though. Great warrior by-and-by, like father. Come back. Talk hard to him."

Na-tee-kah's thoughts followed her hero brother so long as her eyes were open. She had no doubt whatever that he would quickly turn up again with a great heap of new glory. She dreamed of his performing all sorts of marvellous things. All the other boys in camp were planning to catch up and get ahead of him, she knew, for she had heard some of them say so. The Big Tongue had told her of a large number of bears belonging to his record, and he was going on to tell of more when Ha-ha-pah-no overheard and asked him,

"Kill bear all with tongue? Shoot big lie right through? Catch old bear and talk to him; bear die!"

Her tongue was sharp enough, and she strongly sympathized with Na-tee-kah's enthusiasm for Two Arrows. The Big Tongue got away from her and the camp grew more and more quiet.

The spot chosen for it, in a curve of the stream, was one of rare beauty, and the loop formed by the long sweep of the rippling water would have been just the place for a secure corral, if that band of Nez Percés had had any four-footed property to be anxious about. It was not needful to keep a guard over their hope of stealing some thereafter.

CHAPTER XV

A GREAT CAPTAIN

The band of Nez Percés had done very well thus far, and so had the band of white miners, but there had been one other band of travellers which had accomplished a good deal by reason of having an uncommonly good commander.

The wicked old mule that had engineered the stampede of the Nez Percé ponies had continued to hold his position as captain. He could out-kick and out-bray any other mule there, and no mere pony would have dreamed of disputing him. There was some grass to be had, next day after the escape, and there was yet a little water in the pools rapidly drying away, but there was nothing anywhere to tempt to a stoppage. On he went, and on went the rest after him, and the reason why the warriors could not find his trail was because he did not leave any. He obeyed the strong instinct of all large animals, and some smaller ones, to "follow a beaten path and keep in a travelled road." He struck the well-made buffalo trail and did not find any reason for wandering from it. Multitudes of men have a precisely similar instinct, and keep in any particular path in life mainly because they are in it; they stick all the closer if they can see anybody else doing the same thing. That was what the wicked old mule saw, and he may have imagined that the squad or rather string of bisons ahead of him knew where they were going and what for. At all events he led his band closely behind them, and they plodded on in a way that carried them ahead quite rapidly. It carried them into the pass and through it, mule, ponies and all, and there was no one to tell them of what had happened there before or what was about to occur.

Something had happened—something that is pretty sure to come to all bisons, sooner or later. In due season their great bodies reel and fall, and the wolves and buzzards are fed. But for such things the wolves would all die, and they have an unerring judgment as to the condition of an ailing bison. They never attack a healthy bull or cow unless they are in great force and the animal is alone.

The migration of bisons from the parching plain to better pasture had been going on for some time, and the coyotes had followed it as a matter of course. The very day that the old mule halted his runaways at the spring for all the water they could hold, there should have been a painter on the great ledge which was followed by the trail in the middle of the pass. There was a tragedy there worth sketching.

Herd after herd of bisons had gone along that ledge road in clumsy safety, but right there now, at the curve of the projecting rock, stood one who could go no farther. A fragment of an arrow still sticking through one of his hind-legs told what had made him lame in the first place, and the marks of wolf-teeth explained why he had grown lamer and lamer until all he could do was to turn his back to the rock and stand at bay.

Mile after mile of weary walking and painful struggling the poor old beast had contended with the enemies now swarming around him; they had assailed him always from behind, and they had altogether crippled him. His great, terrible head was lowered threateningly, and his deep, sonorous bellow was thick with pain and fury. The watching coyotes sat down or walked around, barking, yelping, howling, snapping their teeth like castanets, sure of a feast to come and hungrily impatient for its beginning. One, hungrier or bolder than the rest, made a rush too soon, and the quick horn of the old bison caught him. Up, up he went, whirling over and over, and his last yelp went down with him into the deep cañon. The head of the bison sank again, and his bloodshot eyes grew filmy; he was faint and sinking, and he swayed staggeringly to and fro. He gave a great lurch forward as his faintness grew upon him, and in an instant he seemed to be all but covered with wolves. They attacked every square foot of him at the same moment, climbing over each other, yelling, tearing, and the bison's time had come. The terror and agony stirred all his remaining life for one last, blinded rush. His instinct was to "charge" and he made one lumbering plunge. The trail at that point afterwards but barely passed the wagon-wheels, and there was no room to spare for the bison's last effort. It bore him heavily, helplessly over the sickening edge, and half a dozen of clinging coyotes went down with him. Hundreds of whirling feet the hunters and the hunted-down bison fell together, to be dashed to pieces upon the rocks at the bottom.

A chorus of howls arose from the remaining wolves, but it did not express pity or horror. Only for a moment did they seem to be in doubt as to what was best to be done. After that it was a wolf-race as to which should first get back to the point at which they could safely clamber and tumble to the bottom of the pass. Their feast had been provided for them, and they ate every part of it, buffalo meat and wolf meat alike, with the help of some buzzards, before Two Arrows or any other human being entered the cañon to disturb them. Then they followed their prospect of further feasting, and it led them on into the grassy valley.

The wicked old mule knew nothing of all this. No coyotes annoyed him or his command, but not a mouthful to eat did they find until they came out where they could see the ancient ruins. At sight of these, hinting of human presence, they halted briefly and then sheered away so as not to approach too nearly so very unpleasant a suggestion. The bisons had led them well, whether or not the mule got the credit of it. Also, there was a fair degree of justification of the instinct concerning beaten paths. New ones may be better, and somebody must hunt them up all the while, but the old roads will do very well for most people until the new ones are fairly mapped out. Christopher Columbus had a hard time of it, and Captain Cook got himself eaten up at last, after finding ever so many new things.

It was a matter of course that the runaways should feel their way farther and farther down the valley, and all sorts of happiness seemed to be before them. Grass, water, nice weather, no masters, no responsibilities, and plenty of good company among themselves. It was a time to grow fat, and to think well of the world they lived in.

The wicked old mule had done his work, but he had gained neither name nor fame by it. He looked sidewise more slyly, whisked his ropy tail more demurely, and kicked his nearest neighbors more viciously than ever. Still, all he or they had gained was a vacation; no work to do for anybody but themselves, but with winter only a few months ahead and with a certainty that wolves, buzzards, coyotes, cougars, grislies, frost, snow-storms, and all the other unknown possibilities of the mountain country were only holding off for a season.

Chapter XVI

VISITING

Two Arrows was treated to an excellent breakfast the morning after his capture. He also saw a white man eat with a knife and fork, and had all the sugar he wanted for the first time. It was a wonderful morning, and a very brilliant pair of eyes were drinking in its marvels greedily.

Rifles, pistols, and all that sort of thing were familiar enough to the young Nez Percé, but he saw new patterns of them and gained tremendous notions of the wealth and skill of the pale-faces who could make such weapons.

"Father," said Sile, "I wish he could read. He's a bright fellow."

"Show him everything you have with a picture in it."

There was no fear that Two Arrows would try to run away after that process began. The printed matter of any sort did not convey to him an idea; it was so much mud; it meant nothing whatever. The pictures were another thing, and Sile had provided himself well with illustrated reading. Two Arrows almost gave up the sullen pride that refused to be astonished, and Sile began to understand "sign language." At all events he nearly twisted himself out of shape in an effort to explain to his captive the nature of ships, cannon, camels, and steam-engines. He felt as if he were a sort of missionary. At last Judge Parks himself handed Two Arrows a photograph of an Indian chief, given him at one of the frontier agencies a few weeks before.

"Ugh! Pawnee!" said Two Arrows.

"I told you so," exclaimed Yellow Pine. "If you showed him dogerrytypes of every tribe there is, he'd name 'em at sight. Jedge, it's about time we set out. I've got a mount ready for him."

Jonas more fully explained to Two Arrows that a visit of peace was planned, and that he was to be marched home again, but the face of the young Indian clouded. That was the one thing he stood in mortal dread of. He thought of the jeers and derision sure to greet him from all other Nez Percé boys when they should see him come home without any glory, and he hung back.

"Mount now," shouted Yellow Pine, with a motion towards the animal he had selected.

A horse! To ride back, instead of returning tired and on foot. That was quite another matter.

"Whoop!" he could not have restrained that yell of relief, and in an instant he was in the saddle. He had been used to riding a barebacked pony, and that made his present outfit the more splendid. All his vanity and ambition came pouring back upon him, and he almost felt as if he had captured that squad of pale-faces and was bringing them in as prisoners. He dashed forward at once, with Sile on one side, Yellow Pine on the other, and the rest following, except a camp-guard of two miners.

Less than an hour later all the Nez Percé band came out under the trees to see what was coming.

"Two Arrows!" almost breathlessly exclaimed Na-tee-kah. "Caught some pale-faces this time."

"Got horse," said Ha-ha-pah-no.

Long Bear and his warriors did not say a word, for they were all but dumb with astonishment from the moment that they recognized the returning wanderer. What would not that remarkable boy do next? Had he killed anybody? Had he really stolen all those white men, or had they stolen him? There he was, anyway, and in a few moments more Yellow Pine and Judge Parks had said "How?" to Long Bear and his best men. Indian manners required that Two Arrows should be silent before his elders until spoken to, but Long Bear almost instantly inquired,

"Where find boy?"

"In camp," said Yellow Pine. "Try to steal horse. Too many pale-face. Catch him. All safe. Big thief some day. Boy now."

All of Two Arrows's dream of glory went out of sight before the grim smiles with which the Nez Percé warriors heard that explanation. They perfectly understood the matter, and that the pale-faces before them wished to be good friends. On their part, they were a good deal more than willing, for they had much to gain from peace and very little from war with mounted riflemen.

"Prisoner?" groaned Na-tee-kah.

"Boy all right," grumbled Ha-ha-pah-no, indignantly. "Find pale-face camp anyhow. Go right in. Old brave all asleep. Never find anything. Big chief by-and-by."

There was some truth in that view of the matter, and Long Bear made a remark that had a little the same sound. At all events Two Arrows was permitted to dismount and walk away, while the conference with his captors went on. In ten seconds he was exhibiting his little hand-mirror to Na-tee-kah and a crowd of other young people, and found his importance coming back to him. None of them had ever ventured to creep, all alone, into a white man's corral. Not a boy or girl among them had such a treasure as the mirror. He had made friends with the pale-faces, at all events. In fact, his standing in that community was rising with tremendous rapidity, until somehow or other the story of his wrestling match with Sile Parks began to be whispered around, and it became necessary for Two Arrows to point at Yellow Pine as the great brave who had really pinioned him. There was not a Nez Percé in the band, old or young, who felt any longing for a grapple with the sinewy, big-boned old miner and all would have been right but for the fact that Two Arrows had not at once escaped from Sile.

NOT A BOY OR GIRL AMONG THEM HAD SUCH A TREASURE AS THAT MIRRORToList

A good understanding was easily established between the miners and the red men, and it was not long before Sile was off his horse and was going around among the young people. He used his eyes as busily as Two Arrows had done, but it is to be doubted if he saw as much, even in what there was to see. It was not long before Na-tee-kah had as good a looking-glass as her brother, and a general distribution of small presents sealed the arrangement that the miners were not to be plundered by that particular band.

"Now, jedge," said Yellow Pine at last, "it's time we moved. S'pose we fetch along that young cub and his sister. Company for Sile. Make the old chief feel fine."

Long Bear gave several grunts of assent when spoken to, and once more Two Arrows felt as if he were growing very fast indeed.

"We'll go back and move the wagons," said Pine to Sile. "You and your young redskin can scout on down the valley. You've got your directions 'bout finding us. Don't go too fast nor too far. The Indian'll smell any danger long before you will. He won't be roped in by anybody in broad daylight, I can tell ye."

He did not look like it as he rode proudly away from the village. Jonas had mounted Na-tee-kah behind him, but Ha-ha-pah-no was to follow the wagons on foot, that the chief's daughter might have somebody to superintend her visit. When Ha-ha-pah-no set out in her turn nearly half the village went with her uninvited, and it took all the authority of Long Bear to keep the other half from keeping them company.

"Come," said Two Arrows to Sile, after a few minutes of silent riding. "We go. Ugh! Shoot a heap."

He had picked up more English words, somehow or other, than he had at first acknowledged, but Sile found it needful to work the sign language pretty industriously for all that.

Na-tee-kah had spent her life in the close retirement of an Indian village. She had been housed up among plains and mountains from all the world, and knew nothing about it. She had lived in a narrower prison than the smallest country village in all the East. The idea of visiting a white man's camp and seeing all there was in it made her tremble all over. She knew her father and ever so many others would be there in an hour or so, and that her wonderful brother had gone on a hunt with the son of the pale-face chief, but she was to enter a strange place with only white warriors for company. It was an awful thing to do, and she could not have done it, nor would Long Bear have consented to it, but for something they both saw in the face of old Judge Parks when he patted her on the head and said,

"Be my daughter a little while. Make a white girl of her for a week. Take good care of her."

Red men have keen eyes for character, and Long Bear understood. So did Na-tee-kah, and yet she would have run away and hidden but for her curiosity, stirred up by what Two Arrows had told her of the contents of that camp and its wagons. An offer to a white girl of a trip to Paris might be something like it, but it would not be much more. Her eyes danced and her fingers tingled as they drew near, and yet the only thing she could see was a couple of commonplace tilted wagons and a lot of horses and mules. The moment she was on the ground the old judge came to her assistance.

"Now, Na-tee-kah, I'll show you something. Come this way."

She stood as straight as an arrow and walked along courageously, but it required all her strength of mind and will to do so. She watched him in silence, as he went into and came out of one of those mysterious rolling tents full of all unknown riches.

"There, now. That'll keep you busy while we're getting ready to move."

She held out both her hands, and when Ha-ha-pah-no at last put her own hand upon her shoulder and said "Ugh!" Na-tee-kah started as if she had been waked from a dream. She had been looking at pictures that told her of another world.

"Heap lie," said Ha-ha-pah-no. "Pale-face tell 'em. Make lie about squaw. There!"

It was a picture of several ladies in evening dress, and Na-tee-kah had been looking at it for five minutes. No such woman as those could possibly be, nor could any human beings get themselves up so wonderfully. It was all a lie, and any intelligent squaw could detect the fraud at a glance.

Na-tee-kah drew a long breath that sounded like a sigh, and just then the shout of Yellow Pine announced that all was ready for a move.

"We'll reach that mine to-morrow night, jedge, if we're lively. Everything's goin' prime now."

With or without an invitation the relatives of Na-tee-kah trudged along with the wagons mile after mile, and Long Bear gained an extra pound of tobacco by sticking to Yellow Pine until the train halted at noon.

Ha-ha-pah-no scolded Na-tee-kah pretty nearly all the way for not knowing more about pale-faces, but she broke down at the noon camp-fire. She undertook to play cook, and in half a minute Jonas discovered that she did not know how to make coffee.

"Wouldn't you have b'iled a black soup?" he exclaimed.

"Poor old squaw!" said Ha-ha-pah-no. "Know all about him. Drink some once; bitter. Put sweet in. Stir him up, so."

"Ugh!" said Na-tee-kah. "Know so much. Ask Two Arrows when he come."

Chapter XVII

MORE FUN

Sile Parks and Two Arrows had the whole valley before them and all the mountains and valleys beyond, and one knew as much about them as did the other. Neither had ever been just there before, and yet the young Nez Percé was at home, and Sile was in a new country. Sile could ride well and he could shoot well, but here at his side was a born hunter. With all sorts of descriptive signs he asked him,

"Did you ever kill a deer?"

"Ugh! heap deer. Heap bear. Heap buffalo. Big heap."

And then all the pride of Two Arrows came to help him explain that he had killed a cougar all alone, and a big-horn and a grisly. By the time he had succeeded in doing so Sile regarded him as a red-skinned wonder, but had so interpreted some of his signs as to include a big snake, a land-turtle, and a kangaroo in the list of asserted victories. It gave him some doubts as to the others, for he said to himself,

"No rabbit can jump as far as he says that thing did. There are no kangaroos here, and they have no horns. I give it up. Maybe he is lying, but he doesn't look so."

Two Arrows was boasting quite truthfully, and the trouble was with Sile's translation.

"Ugh! look. Rifle—"

Sile's eyes followed the pointing finger in vain for a moment. At first he saw nothing but a clump of sumach bushes, but for once he asked no questions. What could be among them? One seemed to move a little. Could it be possible? the horns of a buck!

"Maybe I can hit him. I've heard of such a thing. I'll aim below them; his body is there somewhere."

Two Arrows could have told him just how that deer was standing, but Sile's guess-work was pretty good. He let his rifle-muzzle sink on a line with one of those antlers, and had lowered it a little too much when he pulled the trigger. The kicking of the rifle made the aim a good one, for the sharp report was answered by a great bound from the cover of the sumachs, and in an instant a mortally-wounded buck was dashing across the open, with One-eye close at his heels.

"Ugh! got him," said Two Arrows. "Heap shoot. Bow not so good."

Sile had offered to lend him a rifle at starting, but Two Arrows had prudently refused to disgrace himself. He had never owned one and did not care to show his lack of skill.

That was a fine dash after One-eye and the wounded buck, but it was a short one. The bullet had done its work so thoroughly that there was little trouble left for the dog when he seized his victim's throat to pull him down.

There had been some hunting done by the mining party on their long journey, but Sile could have told Two Arrows if he had chosen to do so, that here lay the first deer he had ever killed. He could also have told him that it appeared to be the largest, fattest, finest, most miraculous buck that anybody in the world had ever killed; as it really was even Two Arrows spoke well of the buck and thought well of the shot which had brought it down.

"If I knew where to find our train I'd take it right in," said Sile, as they hoisted the buck to his own saddle. "I'd just as lief walk."

"Find him," said Two Arrows, understanding the searching look Sile gave towards the mountains. "Go so. Come. Get on horse; ride."

He took the lead at once, but it seemed to Sile that he was going in the wrong direction. He was not at all aware that his friend had skilfully directed their hunt on a line nearly parallel, at no great distance, from that which the train must follow. He was therefore doubly astonished when a brief ride brought them within sight of the wagon-tilts. They had halted, and Sile had double comfort: he could show his father his first deer and he could get a hot dinner, for Ha-ha-pah-no could do very well with a steak if not with coffee.

"Which of you killed the deer?" asked the judge, as they rode in.

Sile was silent long enough for Two Arrows to point at him and remark,

"Heap shoot."

"So I did, father, but he pointed him out. I'd never have seen him if I'd been alone."

"Jest so," said Yellow Pine. "There isn't anything else on the earth like the eyesight of an Indian. I've had 'em sight game more'n once that I'd ha' missed sure."

It puzzled Na-tee-kah somewhat that anybody else should have won anything while her wonderful brother was near by, but Ha-ha-pah-no relieved her by remarking,

"Ugh! The red-head kill deer. Two Arrows show him how. Good."

One of the miners had ridden out from the line of march and returned with another deer, so that fresh venison was plentiful in the camp. Two Arrows felt no longing for any more hunting that day, and he bluntly said so. It was ten times more to his liking to ride along with the train and keep his eyes busy. He was studying white men, and all the world knows what a curious study they are. One white boy was also studying him and his sister, and could not understand them at all. Sile's eyes and thoughts ran about over everything he heard or saw until he almost had a headache.

"Tell you what, father," he said to the judge, "when we go into camp again I'm going to show them my box."

"It's a curiosity box. Show it to them."

The road was necessarily somewhat rough, and wagoning was slow work, and before sunset a place was chosen for an all-night camp. Then came Sile's experiment. He hauled a stoutly-made, leather-covered trunk out of one of the wagons, before the eyes of Two Arrows and Na-tee-kah, and it was instantly evident that neither had ever seen one, but that both understood its use. He unstrapped it, but it did not open, and he made them try it. Lock and key were mysteries they had no thought of, and they almost started back with surprise when Sile pushed a thin bit of steel into one side of that contrivance and all the upper part of it could be tipped right over.

Sile's "box" would have been first-rate rummaging for any boy of his acquaintance, and it was a mine of wonders to the two young savages. He had put into it some things which could hardly be useful to him, even if he should be cast away upon a mountain, as Robinson Crusoe was upon an island, and it was so much the better fun for Two Arrows and Na-tee-kah. The fishing-hooks, lines, reel, etc., made the eyes of the former fairly dance, and Sile brought out a joint-rod and put it together, with a reel on, to show him how the machine worked. Two Arrows grew thoughtful over that affair.

"Big fish break him."

"No. Show you about that to-morrow morning."

"Ugh! ugh!" suddenly exclaimed Ha-ha-pah-no. "Red-head got squaw? Boy!"

He did look young to be married, but she was pointing straight at a brush and comb and some other articles which, to her notion, did not belong in the treasury of a young warrior. Sile at once explained that he used them himself, but there were several brushes and combs, and she added,

"Ugh! Beat squaw. Take 'em away from her. What she do?"

"Try it on," said Sile, handing a brush and comb to Na-tee-kah, and a peal of laughter announced the pleasure of the two Indian ladies, old and young. Even Two Arrows dropped a "spoon-hook" to take an interest in that proceeding.

"Come," said Ha-ha-pah-no, with a long string of merry gutturals of explanation that she had seen a white lady at one of the forts putting up the hair of another. She herself could do it, and in twenty seconds more there was a yell from Na-tee-kah and a tooth out of the comb.

"Let me show you," said Sile, and from that moment there was not one sound from the lips of Na-tee-kah. Whether she was hurt or not nobody knew, for if the comb had extracted hair by the handful she would not have whimpered. Ha-ha-pah-no insisted on having her hair combed by Na-tee-kah. She must know how now, it was evident, and she did, for the comb lost another tooth in the very first tangles of Ha-ha-pah-no's hair.

"That's fun," said Yellow Pine. "Jest look at them critters. That there squaw'll crack that lookin'-glass, twistin' her face, 'fore her combin' is done."

She stood it pretty well, but the other contents of the box had less interest now. She and Na-tee-kah preferred to go on with the brush and comb. Even Two Arrows looked at them so enviously that Sile told him the white chiefs did comb their hair. It was enough. Squaws were made to serve braves, and they were both commanded to take charge of his long, bushy, and decidedly tangled barbering. Not for his life would he have uttered a cry of pain, but he made up his mind that a pale-face can endure a great deal before they got through with him.

Supper had to be eaten, and sharp appetites helped them to get away long enough for that duty, but then the brush and comb began again under Sile's instruction.

"That there comb won't last long," said Yellow Pine. "Tell 'em to put on some grease, Sile, and some ribbons. Ribbons, Sile, and some beads, and—"

"And some red flannel," said Jonas, "and some tinware."

"I'd forgotten all about that," exclaimed Sile, springing up.

In a few moments his visitors were in a new state of excitement, for they were tying up their now glossy locks with brilliant ribbons and strips of gay cloth. To these were added some of the brilliant white-metal ornaments that pass for silver among the very youngest pale-face children. Two Arrows put on his full share of all that was offered and became a very gay-looking young Indian. There was no danger that he would stand on his head and spoil his ribbons, but he felt almost too proud to stand on his feet. He felt more and more sure that the world did not contain quite such another hero, and longed for the presence of his whole band, and of his entire tribe, and of several other tribes, that he might walk up and down in front of them and be admired. No white boy with a new stovepipe hat and a pair of yellow kid gloves ever wanted to walk through so many streets or past quite so many "boarding-schools" as did Two Arrows—only that his showing-off places were such as he was best acquainted with.

Na-tee-kah was more quiet than even Ha-ha-pah-no, for that highly respectable squaw had done up her head remarkably.

"All she wants to finish it off is two tin dippers and a set of sleigh-bells. I saw a squaw do that once. There's no telling what they won't put on. But I say, jedge, that there littler one is a born lady, and she's right down good-lookin' too. All she needs is good dressin' and she'd kind o' shine."

There was not a doubt of it, and her highly-colored ribbons had been put on with better taste than those of Ha-ha-pah-no, and they showed to good advantage her clear, dark complexion, brilliant eyes, and regular features. Old Long Bear had a right to be proud of both his children.

It was grand fun, but there came an end to it at last. Two Arrows went out to share with Sile his camp-watch, and Ha-ha-pah-no and Na-tee-kah were shown to a small tent which had been pitched for them. It was something of a trial to take all that finery away from the admiring blaze of the camp-fire and carry it into the dark hiding-place of that tent, but it had to be done. At all events they could rise early in the morning and comb their hair again and arrange the ribbons and things in some other way.

Na-tee-kah's new world was opening to her wonderfully, and she lay for a long time wide awake, staring into the darkness and trying to imagine pale-face squaws and their ways of doing up their hair and painting themselves and putting on whole heaps of blankets of the most striking colors and patterns.

CHAPTER XIII

TWO WAR-PARTIES

That was a time of uncommon interest and excitement to the entire Nez Percé hunting village. They had plenty to eat and to drink, and some of them had received presents, and the prospect ahead seemed to brighten a little. By nightfall all the warriors were returned from accompanying the mining party, and it was a time for a grand smoke. Some of them had begged Yellow Pine for "fire-water," but not a drop had been obtained. Instead of it they had been informed,

"We're not jest that kind of white men. There isn't a pint of tangle-foot in this 'ere outfit. Ef I want to murder a feller I'll take a rifle to him and do the job clean. I won't go around the bush and massacre him with a whiskey-jug."

The red men understood perfectly well that there was no "fire-water," but that was all they gathered. Plenty of smoking tobacco they did obtain, and it was a grand addition to the dignity of their "council," if every half-naked brave with a pipe in his mouth had a right to consider himself a councillor. They all smoked, and they all wondered what it was best to do next, and they all said so, and every brave among them regretted that it was out of the question for them to acquire possession of the quadrupeds ridden and driven by Judge Parks and his men. The Big Tongue and a few of the younger braves even went so far as to "talk war," but the wiser heads merely grunted at the suggestions volunteered. The Big Tongue had much to say to the smokers nearest him concerning a pale-face warrior whose scalp was among his own treasures. Ha-ha-pah-no was not there to make any sly remarks as to how he actually obtained such a trophy as that and some others on which his reputation as a warrior mainly rested. They sat up until they had smoked all the wisdom out of several pipes of tobacco to each warrior, but did not seem to be any nearer a conclusion. The camp was under the special charge of One-eye, but that dog was becoming quiet and solemn. His especial master had departed, he knew not whither. All the bones in camp now belonged to him, and he had no time to bury so much as one of them. He was not fond of tobacco, and as soon as the smoking began he walked out of camp to patrol the edge of the woods and to keep all the eye left him on duty against possible intruders. He had no faith in a country which was evidently infested by pale-faces.

If he had known more about that valley and the region into which it led, he would have had an even worse opinion of it. The fact that it contained a large stream of water had already suggested many things to the experienced mind of Long Bear. All such water, he well knew, kept on running, no matter what might be its crooks and turnings. If he and his braves could have followed that stream far enough while they were smoking and talking over plans, they might have reached a place where it turned a corner of the mountains and was joined by another and larger stream. The two in partnership were able to float a canoe. There was no canoe afloat there, but there was something yet more important away on down, a pretty long way, below the fork made by the junction of the two streams. There was a camp occupied by red warriors only, without one squaw to be seen in it, and it was therefore the camp of a "war-party." It was accompanied by a large drove of ponies, horses, and mules, and some of these had saddles and others carried packs. These were signs that the war-party had been successful and that pale-faces had been the sufferers. Every quadruped visible wore an air of being more or less fatigued, in token of having been driven or ridden both fast and far. From this it might have been gathered that these red men, however successful had been their expedition, believed or feared that they were followed by somebody whom they preferred to get away from. All these signs told the exact truth; it was also true that some pains had been taken to discover whether or not the supposed pursuit continued.

At the very hour when One-eye was making the best use he could of the bright moonshine in front of his own camp, and knew nothing at all aboutthis other, a tall man stood in the deep shadow of a pine-tree, miles and miles down stream from the resting-place of the war-party. The bridle of a horse hung over his right arm, but the animal stood as motionless as did his master, and both were intently watching a dark shape that rode nearer and could be seen more and more clearly, and that paused at last upon the river-bank within thirty yards. Just as it did so there came from under the shadow of the pine-tree a flash and a sharp report, and all the upper part of the dark shape on the bank fell suddenly to the earth, uttering a loud, fierce yell.

"Got him!" was shouted from under the pine-tree, and the man walked out, leading his horse, while instantly there could be heard the sound of galloping hoofs beyond him. In a minute or so more a stern, hoarse voice rang out.

"Halt! What is it, Garry?"

"Got him, captain. 'Nother of them 'Paches. He won't carry back no news. Dead as a mackerel. Reckon they can't be far away now."

"We've taken pretty good care of their scouts, anyhow."

"Jest so many the less to fight when we come up with 'em. They'll outnumber us bad enough, I reckon, best we can make of it."

"Back to camp, Garry. Corporal Peters, take the same post, with two men. There may be more of them."

"All right, captain."

There was a little more talking done, but these seemed to be a somewhat quiet set of men. There were six of them besides the captain. They were all dressed in blue, and wore brass buttons and carried short-barrelled carbines and sabres. A good look at them would have recalled to the mind of Two Arrows all the arguments he had ever heard as to the wisdom of keeping the peace with the pale-faces. When they reached the camp, after "changing the guard" at Garry's river-side post, it was easy to see that their entire force consisted of several times as many men of the same sort. Every man was on his feet, wide awake and waiting for orders. One squad of five stood with each man's hand upon the bridle of a saddled horse, ready to mount, just as the first squad must have been, when it heard the warning report of Garry's carbine. A company of United States cavalry, veteran Indian fighters, following a "hot trail," keeps itself wonderfully ready for action. It is not easy to take such men by surprise. Now, however, at the word of command, all was instantly quiet again. The actual meaning of the alarm was rapidly told from man to man, and several remarked:

"Good for Garry! We'll catch 'em yet."

All who had a right to go to sleep, did so as unconcernedly as if they had been in a hotel. On the whole, it looked as if something else than peace were on its way into the valley where One-eye was keeping watch for the smokers. The last man to lie down was the captain, and one of the wide-awake squad nodded at him and said to another,

"If there was forty alarms 'fore sun-up, old Grover'd be the first man to turn out every time."

"Not much reg'lation 'bout him."

"But there's lots of fight."

"He can get more hard work out of men and hosses, and he can do more himself, and he can sleep less, and say less about it all, than any other captain I ever served under."

That, therefore, was the kind of soldiers from whom the Apaches were wisely trying to get away, and Garry's carbine had destroyed their prospect of learning how very near he and his might be. It looked very much as if two days more of hard riding would bring them into a sort of trap, with the mountains before and the cavalry behind. Still, even then, there would be the pass, if they knew where to find it. There also were One-eye and all of his men and Sile Parks and his party; and the wicked old mule, too, with his command, was in the valley somewhere. Only a few days earlier the entire sweep of forest and "open and mountain-side" had been unoccupied by anything more dangerous or more interesting than wild game and the wild animals that fed on it. It is very curious how suddenly immigrants will sometimes pour into a new country if there is a good trail pointing out the way.

The spot chosen by Yellow Pine for the camp of the mining party was by a dancing little brook which came down from the mountain to the right of them, and the path by which they travelled that day had barely kept them outside of the rocky slopes. Some coyotes came prowling around, to yelp over the faint smell of roasted meat that floated out to them from the camp-fires. Once during the night the cry of a wandering cougar came wailing through the silence and was followed by that of a horned owl who had noiselessly flapped near enough to blink his great eyes at the blaze. For all that, it was the loneliest kind of a place, and the hours went by until sunrise without the smallest real disturbance or hint of perils to come.

Judge Parks himself was on the watch in the first gray of dawn, and the camp was dim enough even after there were rosy tints upon the distant mountain summits. He stood gazing at these and leaning upon his rifle, when Yellow Pine walked out to take his customary survey of matters.

"We're going to have a fine day, jedge."

"Splendid weather. Pine, just think of all this magnificent country as it will be when it's settled. Farms, towns, villages, mines, railways, factories—"

"There won't be any game, then, or any red Indians, either."

"There isn't a finer country in all the world. The new time is coming, Pine."

"Of course it is. Our mine's coming first thing. We'll get there 'fore sundown. Wish I knew what else was coming."

"Afraid of anything?"

"Got a curious feeling in my back. Always have it when there's something up. It's as much like the rheumatiz as it is like anything."

"Guess that's what it is, then."

"I dunno 'bout that. I've had all sorts of things happen when I had this 'ere feeling onto me."

"Exactly, Pine. I've had dinner happen to me a good many times just when I had a sort of feeling it was coming. Soon as I got right down hungry I knew it was a sure sign. I say, look at those boys."

"Going a-fishing. I'd call it—Well, it's a good thing for 'em to do. They can't miss bringing in a good string. Sile, see here."

"Halloo!"

"Get back with some for breakfast if you can. We'll be right here till the critters have done feeding. Catch a heap."

"All right," shouted Sile. "He says the water's full of 'em."

"Of course it is."

"Sile," said his father, "don't throw away your time on fly-fishing. Use bait, and pull 'em right in. They'll bite."

"I'm going to spoon for 'em. Can't find any bait."

"Never mind, jedge," said Pine. "I've seen trout in some of these mountain streams jump for a bare hook quick as it tetched the water. There's too many on 'em, and they get the hungriest kind."

"They won't mind much what they jump at, that's sure. I must say I'd like some for breakfast, though."

Yellow Pine and the judge had other matters on hand, and the latter had a short nap to take, after his "watch." The animals had to be cared for, moreover, before any mere human being had a right to be fed.

The first noise that was made in camp brought Na-tee-kah and Ha-ha-pah-no out of their tent, comb and brush in hand. They both made sure of their ribbons and that all was in order before they had a word to say to anybody. It could not be denied that they were a very bright looking and highly ornamented pair, Ha-ha-pah-no being perhaps a little ahead.

Chapter XIX

WONDERFUL FISHING

There had been a good deal of discussion of the fishing question between the two young friends, for Two Arrows knew nothing of the powers of a "spoon-hook." Sile had them of several sizes, and Two Arrows admitted to himself that anything so very bright and pretty must have special effectiveness. Any of those spoons was brilliant enough to have been worn in the hat of a great chief, but the doubt remaining was as to what the trout would think of them. The gaudy assortment of artificial flies Two Arrows quite turned up his nose at. The fish of the western mountains were not in the habit of biting at such things, and could not be taught to do so. As to the hooks, however, large and small, anybody could see their superiority over such as he was accustomed to using, and the lines were elegant. Sile provided him with a rod, and when he marched away with it he felt a strong desire to carry it to and through his own camp, that everybody he knew might see what an extraordinary thing he was doing. No Nez Percé boy that he had ever heard of had been able to go a-fishing with a joint-rod and a spoon-hook.

They had but a mile or so to walk in order to reach the nearest bend of the little river, and they startled more than one gang of deer on the way. Sile had his rifle and Two Arrows had his bow, but the morning had been given up to fish, and they stuck to their original purpose in spite of all temptation. On the bank of the stream they paused for a moment and took a survey of the situation. The water was not more than fifty yards wide, and did not seem to be deep, but it ran with rippling swiftness.

"That'll do," said Sile. "It's plenty strong enough to carry a spoon. You won't have to skitter it a bit."

"Ugh! Heap fish," said Two Arrows, but he did not understand Sile's remark and wondered what was to come next. During all his life thus far he had never thought of the pale-faces as fishermen, or that they really knew anything valuable about such matters. The contents of Sile's box had staggered him, and now he looked on in silence while the "Red-head" (as Ha-ha-pah-no had named him) put his rod together, setting the reel firmly in its socket, and then deftly fitted on the spoon-hook with its fine wire "snell." Sile's father was an enthusiastic fisherman and had given his son more than a little good schooling. Up went the rod, and the line swing lightly back for a second, and then, with a perfect cast, the brilliant "spoon" flew over the water and alighted among the swift ripples. The current caught it and whirled it away, the polished silver glittering and dancing near the surface, but it was visible only for an instant. There came a rush and a plunge, and away out of the water sprang a splendid trout with Sile's hook fastened firmly in his too hasty jaw.

"Hurrah!" shouted Sile. "Got him!"

"Ugh! Good," said Two Arrows. "Break!"

"No, he won't break any line. See!"

Two Arrows did see a great deal in a very few moments. The tough rod bent, and Sile gave a little line at first; but the trout made an up-stream rush and was guided to the shore. He was lying on the grass, quietly enough, just after that. So was another and another, and now Two Arrows had mastered the idea and was at work with energy. It surprised Sile to see how perfectly his red friend could handle his new tools, but it was well that the rod was a stout one, for the reel and its uses were as yet an enigma. It was exciting sport, for there was hardly any waiting for bites whatever. The trout were on the lookout for their breakfasts, and nobody had ever before offered them such attractive little silvery fish as they now saw, every now and then struggling through the water, all ready to be seized upon.

It was a great lesson to Two Arrows, and it promised a capital breakfast to the mining party.

"Guess we've got enough," said Sile at last. "We'd better hurry back to camp."

At that moment a strange and unexpected sound came to his ears from some point lower down the stream, and Two Arrows came near to dropping his rod into the water.

"Ugh! Catch now!"

"Yes, you've caught your fish, but what's that? It sounds for all the world like a mule braying."

"Two Arrows know him. Heap bad mule. Nez Percé lose all pony. Find 'em now. Red-head come?"

Sile looked with admiration upon the fiercely excited face of the young Nez Percé. The dark eyes fairly glittered with pleasure and expectation, and he was striving, with all the words and signs he was master of, to convey an idea of the loss his band had sustained, and now once more, and more sonorously, the "morning bugle" of a mule in command of something came ringing up the river.

"I'll string the trout," said Sile, as he began to do so, "then I'll go with you.

It'll be grand if we can really catch them."

"Two Arrows catch 'em all, heap time. Get one, get all tribe."

"Wish we were mounted. Better go to camp and get some horses."

"Ugh! No wait. Find now."

There was no such thing as resisting his eager urgency, and Sile himself began to get excited. The trout made two magnificent "strings," but were pretty heavy to carry, and it was decided to hang them and the two rods upon the limb of a tree until a visit should have been paid to the owner of that bray. All this was quickly attended to, and then the two fishermen were instantly changed into pony-hunters.

Not even his adventure with the grisly, or his timely success with the two bisons when his people were starving, had so aroused the ambition of Two Arrows. The future fortunes of his entire band seemed to him to depend once more upon his own individual good-conduct. Sile thought he had never seen so proud looking a human being.

The speckled beauties from the river swung heavily from the high but bending branch as the two boys hurried away, but these were almost forgotten by both in the course of a few minutes. They did not have to follow far the windings of the stream before Two Arrows, who was somewhat in the advance, dodged behind a tree and beckoned eagerly to Sile:

"Ugh! Look! Pony!"

Just beyond him was a grassy glade glistening with morning dew, and scattered over it was the entire command of the wicked old mule, the wealth and the comfort together of the Nez Percé pony-riders. To have been seen by them prematurely would have been a pretty sure way of stampeding them again, and the occasion called for prudence and good management. Some of the animals still had their long hide lariats hanging and dragging from their necks and some had not, but Two Arrows noted one of the former, a very good-looking pony, feeding at no great distance from a clump of hazel and willows beyond him. He made Sile understand his purpose of getting into that cover, and then all that Sile had to do was to watch him. Down dropped the young Nez Percé, and from that moment there was little of him to be seen, except when his gayly ribboned head now and then showed itself, peering over the wet, luxuriant grass and weeds. Then a slight movement among the willows told of his safe arrival, and still the runaways were feeding quietly, unaware of the nearness of human beings or other enemies. Sile peered from behind his tree and watched the movements of the particular pony his friend had pointed out. He was a brisk sort of fellow, and he was working at his breakfast busily. Nearer and nearer he fed his way towards a projecting growth of the hazel-bushes and Sile perceived a promising shake in one of these. There was something more than a shake hidden by them, for in about one minute more a light, lithe, graceful human form sprang suddenly out. A quick grasp at the trailing lariat, a rapid twist of a loop of it around the animal's face, a buoyant leap, and Two Arrows was a mounted Indian once more. Every beast of the wicked old mule's startled command was familiar with the tones of the whoop of triumph which called them all away from their grass and their freedom. They had many a time been driven in from other pastures by that particular yell, and it seemed now as if each of them took a swift look around him and listened for the expected voice of One-eye. It should naturally have followed that whoop. After that it was as if they had only been waiting for somebody to come, and wished to say as much. Their commander put out his head and brayed lustily, and so did all the other mules, but the ponies took the matter more soberly. Whether or not they had already begun to discover warning signs of cougars, wolves, grislies and other insecurities of their situation, they actually felt better to be once more in the company of a human being whom they knew. Sile wondered greatly to see how readily the whole drove obeyed the shouts of Two Arrows, and permitted themselves to be gathered and driven. He refused the invitation given him to mount one of the ponies, for he had doubts of his success in managing it barebacked and with such a halter-bridle. He explained as well as he could that he preferred to carry the fish and the rods and the news to his own camp, leaving Two Arrows to handle his captives as best he could. That was just what Two Arrows wanted. He was almost afraid lest the pale-faces should send him some help and so take from him part of the glory of his fresh achievement. There was little danger of that, as Sile was soon to discover. He hurried back after his fish in a state of such excitement that he very nearly forgot that he was in a new country. He would have forgotten it more completely if it had not been for something he heard as he drew nearer the spot where he had left his speckled game.

"What's that?" he suddenly exclaimed, stopping short and listening. "What's all that growling? I never heard a bear, but it might be one."

So it might be, indeed, in a country where they were so plentiful, but it was not a grisly this time. It was only a common black bear, very fond of fish, and tremendously disgusted at the failure of his efforts to get hold of some which had plainly been caught and left expressly for him. Standing upon his hind-feet, and springing up as far as he was able, his paws just reached the end of the longest string of trout and set it a swinging. Two Arrows had wisely insisted upon bending down a branch and hanging the fish pretty high, Indian fashion, and Sile now saw the reason of it.

"He'd bring 'em all down as it is if I should let him take his time to it. What shall I do now? Oh, but ain't I glad I brought along my rifle!"

He was glad of it, very; but when he raised it in the direction of that bear the sight seemed to dance in all directions, and he could not get a good aim, short as was the distance.

Sile had the "buck ague."

Even old hunters sometimes find their nerves playing tricks on them. It would not do to miss a shot then and there, and Sile lowered his rifle.

"I'll try a rest and see about this thing. I must hit that bear in the head the first time, sure." He stepped behind a tree and put his rifle through the crotch of a projecting branch. That tree had no shake in it; and the barrel grew steady. "He is getting up on his hind-feet again. Now for him."

The bear poised himself, with uplifted head, and, just as he lifted his paw for another scratch at the fish, Sile pulled the trigger.

The range was very short, the rest was a good one, the sight was quick but careful, and the bit of lead went straight to its intended place under the ear of that black bear. He would need no more fish from that time forth, and he pitched heavily forward upon the ground.

"Wait a moment, Sile! Never run in on a b'ar till yer sure of him. Reckon he's dead, though. Stand where you are, my boy!"

"Why, father! Yellow Pine! You here? I never expected to see you."

"Well, my son," said the judge, "we thought we'd come over and see what luck you were having. Where's Two Arrows?"

"We watched ye jest a moment," said Pine. "Allers take sight from a rest if you can get one. You did that thing fine. There's the making of a prime good shot in ye."

"I shook all over at first," said Sile, walking a little nearer the bear.

"Buck ager. I've had it. He won't come to. If he does it's no matter, now we've got here. I'll come back after breakfast with a hoss and fetch him in. Where's the redskin?"

Sile rapidly explained the cause of his delay in getting back to camp; but what he did not know or explain was the fact that the Nez Percés had had no idea that their drove of lost ponies had wandered into that valley.

"Glad they've got 'em," said Yellow Pine. "Every hoof of ourn'll be safer from this time on, treaty or no treaty, good Indians or bad."

“Would they really steal from us, after all?” asked Sile, soberly.

“Steal hosses? Well, now, that isn’t jest the way it looks to them. They’re brought up to it. All hoss-flesh is fair game to a plains redskin. The more they have of their own, the easier it is to get ‘em to keep their hands off from them that you have and to make believe good. These ‘ere Nez Percés ain’t a bad lot. Hope we won’t run afoul of any that’s worse than they are, and more of ‘em.”

Sile was proud of his fish, and tenfold prouder of his bear, but the proudest person in the mining-camp that morning was Na-tee-kah. Her wonderful brother had earned some more glory. The next proudest being was probably Ha-ha-pah-no, and she asked, several times in succession, of both herself and Na-tee-kah, and without any satisfactory answer,

“What Big Tongue say, now? Tell how he caught pony?”

Chapter XX
A FULL CORRAL

Two arrows was a born horseman. About the earliest memory he had was of riding rather than walking. The pony he was now on was one which had carried him many a time. As soon as he had cut and trimmed a very long and serviceable tree-branch all the other ponies and the mules perfectly understood what it was for.

He was in a serious hurry. It was the most important affair of his life. So far as he could see, the only ponies now missing from the drove were the ones which had not been stampeded, but had remained in camp to be eaten. All the rest had been rescued and kept in good order by the genius and generalship of the wicked old mule. Two Arrows could but wish that a dozen or so of the best dogs had been stampeded at the same time. He rode busily hither and thither, shouting vigorously and lashing his charges away from every tuft of grass they lingered over. He knew exactly where to find his people, and he meant to find them quickly. The distance was nearly the same that had been travelled the day before by the mining party, but the loaded wagons had taken more time upon it than loose ponies would, followed by an excited boy with a long "gad."

The fact that he had eaten no breakfast was one which hardly occurred to Two Arrows, in his eager determination to get his runaways home in the shortest possible order. Once they were headed in the right direction there was but little difficulty in guiding them rightly, and now the old mule took his accustomed place in the advance. It was as if he had repented and was even willing to get some credit for leading his reformed command in the way they should go.

The Nez Percé community had all eaten a good breakfast that morning; there had been no vegetables, to be sure, but not a soul had missed them. With plenty of fish and fresh meat they had all that red Indians expect to be provided with, and they asked for no more. Their kind of human life can be kept a-going upon a very narrow diet. The laziest brave in camp was well fed, but for all that there was a general air of dejection and despondency. Long Bear himself sat in front of his lodge, cross-legged and moody, all the forenoon: his children were away from him, on a visit to the pale-faces; his ponies were away upon another visit, he could not guess with whom; his dogs, with the solitary exception of One-eye, had all visited the camp-kettles. His only remaining consolation seemed to be his pipe, and he was rapidly and extravagantly using up all the tobacco he had obtained from Yellow Pine. The shadow of the mighty maple near him grew shorter until it had little more left to lose and could almost announce the arrival of midday. Just then there arose, at the edge of the woods, a long, ear-piercing howl, followed by such a volley of yelps and barking as can only be fired off by a very remarkable dog. One-eye was informing the camp that something great was drawing near, and was doing his best to make up for the absence of the other dogs.

The Nez Percé warriors went for their weapons instinctively but somewhat listlessly, until they heard a tremendous whoop join in with the barking of One-eye and recognized the powerful voice of the Big Tongue. He could out-whoop any other brave he knew of, and he was now doing his best. He had been strolling out towards the open country when One-eye began, and had found and seized upon a sudden heap of unexpected glory.

Away in advance of his command, farther and farther, had wisely trotted the long-legged, long-eared, long-absent wicked old mule. Not another quadruped was in sight when One-eye gave the alarm. The Big Tongue bounded forward as if he were charging upon a beaten enemy, and the mule did but whinny affectionately when he caught the remains of the lariat at the place where it had been gnawed asunder, and sprang triumphantly upon the back of the recaptured mule.

Whoop followed whoop as the happy warrior rode his prize towards the camp, and the entire band, squaws and children included, poured out under the trees to rejoice that they now had a mule as well as a dog. Long Bear came among the rest. Ha-ha-pah-no was not there to make unpleasant remarks, but the old chief knew that mule very well and he knew that by no chance had he returned to his owners of his own free will. He would have remained more contentedly with a man who had found or stolen him. Long Bear was positive that he had not followed his masters lovingly across the mountains, and that he need not make any pretence of having done so. He could hardly have believed that the mule was there at all but that he could see him, with the Big Tongue sitting upon him to be admired.

The old chief turned and looked keenly and wistfully across the grassy rolls, and so did several others of the wiser warriors. There was quite a rise of ground at a little distance and One-eye was making for it as fast as his legs could carry him. Suddenly, as if by a common impulse, all the woods rang with a full chorus of whooping. Over the crest of that green ridge came galloping pony after pony and mule after mule, in a confused rush, and then a shrill shout arose beyond, and they could shortly see Two Arrows, gayly ribboned, ornamented, mounted, dashing madly back and forth and lashing forward the rear-guard of that battalion.

Long Bear folded his arms and stood erect and still, as if he were trying to hold himself in. His own boy, and therefore he himself, had done another mighty deed.

"Ugh! Two Arrows! Young chief! Find pony all alone."

The Big Tongue tried hard to look as if he had found the mule, but it did not seem to fit, somehow, and twice he opened his mouth widely and shut it again in silence; there was no whoop ready to come. Every other brave had a score or more quite ready, but Two Arrows grew silent as he came nearer and rode more sedately. There was almost an air of stateliness about him when at last he followed the trail of his important cavalcade in under the shadows of the forest.

It was not becoming for him to volunteer, in boyish haste, an explanation of his utterly unlooked-for exploit. Even the gray-heads felt that he was entitled to a respectful and dignified reception, and Long Bear himself stepped forward and inquired, in due form, precisely how that wonderful rescue had been accomplished. Now that the question was asked of him, Two Arrows was willing enough to tell the entire story, and to point to all the animals as witnesses to the truth of it. As fast as he told it, the more or less distorted facts went swiftly round from lip to lip among the squaws and younger people. It was almost unlucky for the Big Tongue to remark, dignifiedly,

"Boy find pony. Warrior ride him;" for a half-grown warrior near him added,

"Boy *there*. Big Tongue *here*. Same way hunt buffalo."

It sounded a little like Ha-ha-pah-no, and the Big Tongue was silenced. He and the rest now listened to the answers of Two Arrows as to his visit, and he gave a full account of the good treatment he had received. It looked as if honors had fairly been heaped upon him and Na-tee-kah, and, for their sakes, upon Ha-ha-pah-no. Some of the older squaws shortly picked up the annoying fact concerning the latter that she had learned how to make coffee, and that her hair was now brushed and combed and made shiny. They knew what combs were. She would probably wear one now. She would never again be the same woman in her own estimation, they were sure of that. She had always held her head high enough, for her husband was a renowned brave and her tongue was always in good order.

The drove of ponies and mules was the centre of attraction, after Two Arrows had finished his recital, and every Nez Percé searched it eagerly for his own. It was decided to send off several braves at once, with some squaws and pack-ponies, to bring through the pass the lodges and other materials they had hidden near the camp of their starvation. Two Arrows ate his breakfast and dinner in one meal, and was then bidden to mount a pony at once and ride away after his pale-face friends, with the strongest assurances that the Nez Percés regarded them as so many brothers. Long Bear also sent a handsome cougar-skin to Sile, as a proper acknowledgment of the fact that he had been a looker-on at the rescue of the quadrupeds from the misguiding leadership of the bad old mule. Two Arrows rode gladly away upon his errand, and some of the braves set out at once after the "left baggage." All whom they left behind them had now abundant subject-matter for conversation and for unlimited "Ughs!" The entire future suddenly brightened up for that band of Nez Percés, and they were entirely confident of their ability to procure a new supply of dogs. As for One-eye, that sagacious brute wandered around the corral, from hoof to hoof, until he knew the facts of the case thoroughly. He would have followed Two Arrows, but for the stern refusal of Long Bear. He was needed at home all the more now that there would be additional watching and barking to be done. On the whole he was as well satisfied to have it so, for his accumulation of bone treasures was becoming an affair for any dog to think about seriously.

Sile was not exactly a hero when he reached camp, but he was an uncommonly hungry boy. It seemed to him that he could eat as many trout as Ha-ha-pah-no could broil for him, and he certainly worked at it steadily for a long time. Every other human being in camp did the same, although some had already made a fair beginning upon venison cuts and coffee. All had room for some fresh trout, and all said they would be glad of a little bear-meat for a change. Sile was in the saddle promptly enough after breakfast, to go and see his bear brought in. He would not willingly have missed that, and was only afraid lest it should have been stolen in his absence, in spite of the care taken by Yellow Pine to throw bushes over it, and give any roving coyote an idea that a trap was there. Said Pine, in answer to a question,

"Them critters is too cunnin' for their own good. One on 'em'd sit down in front of that there, and howl all day and all night before he'd make up his mind to scratch at the brush."

"How'd he guess at a trap?"

"Oh, they're laid on kind o' reg'lar, and he'd smell the b'ar too, and he'd know it was somethin' more than ordinary. There's jest one thing they ain't cunnin' enough for, and that's a rifle-bullet. They'd dodge that if they could see it a comin'."

The bear was found all safe and was brought in and skinned, and Sile said to himself,

"Now I've got something better than a deer to tell of when Two Arrows gets back again."

Chapter XXI

THE GOLD MINE

A proud girl was Na-tee-kah that bright September day, and she took an extraordinary amount of pains with her hair. So, for that matter, did Ha-ha-pah-no, and Sile could but discern that both treated him with much more respect than at first. He had been with Two Arrows at the recovery of the ponies, he had killed a buck and a bear, and was evidently able to use the weapons of grown-up white braves. He was therefore not a boy to be snubbed; and, if it had not been for his unfortunate light complexion, he was almost good-looking. At all events he was disposed to do his best to be polite, and they were willing to meet him as nearly half-way as was consistent with dignity and propriety. They were under the especial care of the judge himself, however, and Na-tee-kah derived a vast amount of comfort from an occasional look at his very fatherly and benevolent face. Her obvious respect for Yellow Pine was mingled with something like fear as yet, and she would not have a word to say to any of the miners. Horses were furnished to both of them when the camp broke up for the day's travelling, and no man in the party was more at home upon one, except that a side-saddle was an invention that they had never heard of and did not need.

"We'll git to the mine afore night, jedge," said Yellow Pine, when they halted for their noon luncheon, and the further information he added stimulated all hands to push forward. Not one sign of peril or even of human presence, other than their own, did they encounter, and yet the other human beings of that region were hourly drawing nearer.

The camp of the Apache marauders broke up at sunrise, with a considerable amount of discontented grumbling. A man familiar with their dialect, or with only a little of it, could easily have gathered that they were eager for news which did not come, and for scouts who did not return. Not all of them, to say the least, would ever again come into that or any other camp, news or no news. In the absence of any, it was plainly a due precaution to push forward even farther beyond the supposed pursuit of the men in blue.

There was a good deal more than a mere supposition about that pursuit, for Captain Grover and his men were on the trail at as early an hour as was consistent with a proper care of their horses, and a hearty breakfast all around. They were a fine looking lot of men, bronzed and weather-beaten and soldierly. Their uniforms were not exactly in "parade" condition, but there was nothing slovenly about them, and their weapons were in excellent order.

They had several "led-horses," to make good the places of any that might become over-wearied, and every animal in the troop showed signs of careful grooming. A captain, a lieutenant, and thirty men did not seem an overpowering force for a hundred and more of Apache warriors to run from, but neither of the two parties could have a correct knowledge of the strength of the other. Besides, the main object of an Indian raid is never a hard fight, but rather to pick up scalps and plunder and get away without serious loss. Red men are courageous enough, but they have a strong objection to being shot at or sabred, and know that it does not take a great many hard-won victories over cavalry, even if they should win them, to about wipe out the fighting strength of a tribe.

As for Captain Grover, he had been ordered to follow and "strike" that band of Apaches, and compel them to return to their "reservation," and he had no other purpose in mind than to obey thoroughly.

"I'll follow them," he remarked to the lieutenant, "as far as they choose to go. We've wiped out six of their scouts already."

"Garry," said one of the men at the same moment, "reckon them 'Paches'll begin to think this 'ere's an unhealthy crowd to creep in on."

"The more on 'em we can pick off," said Garry, "the fewer we'll have to fight at the close."

"Sharp work when that comes, or I'm mistaken, but they can't take hoss plunder into the mountains."

As they rode along so cheerily and confidently, it became plainer and plainer that those men had small doubt of their ability to deal with any ordinary band of red horse-thieves if they could meet them fairly. It would hardly have seemed so to an unprejudiced observer of the Apache cavalcade that morning. Every warrior was a perfect horseman, and was well mounted and well armed. There were lances instead of sabres, but the pistols and carbines, or rifles, were just as good as those carried by the cavalry. The red men were all trained and experienced soldiers, under capable leaders, and it looked as if all they had to do was to choose a good position and wait for Captain Grover and his men, and destroy them all. As it was, all they seemed to think of was to urge their drove of stolen quadrupeds forward. They could not make the best of time so encumbered, and when they again halted for the night, the men in blue were several miles nearer without one Apache knowing exactly where they were. The trail these had made told Captain Grover all he as yet needed to know, with the help of one used-up pony that the Indians had turned loose to shift for himself.

"Beginning to break down, are they?" said the captain. "I'll strike them among the foothills of the ranges within three days."

All that exciting chase was as yet hidden from the red and white men in the upper valley, and it was quite possible that they would never know anything about it. That depended, in fact, upon whether the Apaches should turn to the left or the right when they reached the "forks" of the little river.

It was pretty late when Two Arrows again caught up with his pale-face friends, and his pony showed signs of very hard riding. If he had been a grown-up brave he could not possibly have had so warm a reception, except from Na-tee-kah and Ha-ha-pah-no. These two considered him the tallest kind of a young chief already, but all the rest regarded him very much as Yellow Pine did, as "the likeliest young redskin he'd ever come across."

"I believe he is," said Judge Parks, and Sile had added,

"Father, what wouldn't he know pretty soon if he could learn to read and write? He understands everything he sees right away."

"I'd like to try the experiment, Sile, but I don't believe he would ever take kindly to books. I'll talk about it some other time. There is something else on my mind just now."

There was a good deal upon everybody's mind, and even Sile ceased to admire Long Bear's present when Yellow Pine rose in his stirrups and pointed forward, shouting.

"There she is, jedge—right back in that there notch!"

Away to the right of them the craggy mountain arose against the sky, facing the valley with an uncommonly precipitous wall. In this grim face of granite could be seen what looked like a mere indentation. When they came to it, however, they discovered that Yellow Pine's "notch" was much narrower at its mouth than beyond it, owing to some ancient overturn and "landslide" of great rocks and small, which almost shut it in. Beyond this barrier, the opening through which was a mere roadway, there were several acres of good grass and trees. There were springs of water also, and the whole place was a good one to camp in, so long as no more bowlders should break loose from the slopes above and come crashing down into it. It was plain that none had done so for a long time past, and the wagons were hauled fearlessly in. There was nobody with them but their drivers, for every other human being had galloped on after Yellow Pine and Judge Parks until the old miner drew rein in front of a great mass of shattered, ragged, dirty looking quartz rock. In front of this a deep hole had been dug by somebody, and near it were traces of old camp-fires, bones of deer and buffalo, some rusty tin cans, and a worn-out pickaxe.

"That's the lode, jedge. It's all I ever told ye it was. Safest place in the world, too, now the 'Paches are gethered onto their reservation. We can go right to work to-morrow mornin'."

Judge Parks was at that moment examining some bits of quartz he had picked up. He took from his pocket a magnifying-glass and closely inspected stone after stone.

"It looks like it, Pine. I haven't a doubt of the value of that vein. Look at that, Sile."

Sile looked with a face more deeply flushed than even his father's.

"Why, it's exactly like Yellow Pine's old specimens, so far as I can see; no more gold in these than in them."

"That's just the point, Sile. He brought me fair specimens. There isn't any humbug or delusion about it. It's all right, Pine, so far as I can see. As for safety, the mouth of this notch could be made a perfect fort of, if we had to quit mining and go to fighting."

"Guess we won't ever have to do that. Game's plenty, and so is fish, and we won't have to use up our provisions. Chance for you, Sile. You can keep the camp-fires going. Fetch in some fish, first thing in the morning, and then go for all the fresh meat there is. What we don't eat we can cure and put away."

"I'll do the hunting!" shouted Sile. "What are the men all chopping for? There's plenty of dry dead wood."

"I'd call it!" exclaimed Yellow Pine. "If they ain't struck with the mine-fever now. Jest look at 'em, jedge."

"Pine," shouted one of the men from a little distance, "this 'ere shelf by the spring's the spot you marked for the shelter, isn't it?"

"All right, boys," he responded. "Thirty feet by twelve, and an ell for cooking and an ell for stowage."

"Nine feet high to the front, and slope to seven and a half, and lay on the mud as you go?"

"That's it. Pitch in, boys."

"I declare," said the judge; "they haven't eaten a mouthful and they've begun building."

"They're old hands, and the sight of that show of pay-rock has kind o' stirred 'em up. It's all correct, though, jedge. We can look for storms every now and then, and the shelter won't be up any too soon if one of them busters should happen to be on its way."

CHAPTER XXII

A NEW SETTLEMENT

There is nothing else like enthusiasm. That band of bearded miners went into their work like a crowd of boys building a snow fort. Ha-ha-pah-no and Na-tee-kah took full possession of the camp-fires and cooked for dear life. Judge Parks and Yellow Pine finished their inspection of the hole in the rock and of the ore which had been dug out of it, and then they went to help Sile and Two Arrows care for the horses and mules.

"We won't unpack much till the house is up," said the judge.

"You're satisfied with the outcrop, are ye?" asked Pine, a little proudly.

"It's all you said it was, and that is all I could ask for. We can run a tunnel right in now, so we can work straight along, under cover, in bad weather."

"That's the thing to do. I believe it will pay for itself from the very start."

"If it does," said the judge, "it will be an uncommonly good mine for a gold-mine. Not one in ten but what empties the pocket of its first owner."

"This one won't, then. It's as good a property as there is, and we can cover all the ledge with claims and get a good title to 'em. It's fresh ground, and no kind of interference—"

"Unless the Apaches interfere."

"They don't often come east so far as this, 'specially now that most of 'em have been cornered. Mining in these parts isn't the risky kind of business it used to be. Must say, though, that I felt kind o' streaked sometimes, last year, when I was a prospectin'."

"There was risk in it, all alone; but nine rifles and a good breastwork will make a tremendous difference."

"They will that, and there's no sech thing as takin' us in the rear. They can't climb over that ridge, nor that one."

It was later than usual when anybody lay down that evening. Two Arrows and his sister had heard of mines before, but they had never seen one, and the whole matter was a great curiosity.

These uncommonly well-behaved pale-faces meant to dig a hole into the side of that mountain and get gold out of it, and they were going to build a stone "lodge" and stay there. Sile explained to them, as well as he could, a purpose he had formed of making a great farm in that valley, and raising all sorts of things to feed the miners, and of having a town there, with schools and churches for the Indians, and a public library and a saw-mill and a grist-mill and a blacksmith-shop and a hotel. The main idea obtained by Two Arrows was that in a little while the valley would be full of horses of the best kinds. Na-tee-kah went beyond that and got a picture into her mind of a big stone lodge, where a trader would live and have for sale a wonderful heap of all such things as the white squaws dressed themselves up with. She went to sleep at last, with her black eyes half dazzled by a vision of bright colors and glitterings, and had a dream that the trader had come and was ready to trade almost anything for the skin of a grisly bear. As for Two Arrows, not all that could be said about mines and farms could drive from him one grand ambition, that had taken deep root as he studied the many possessions of those pale-faces. Somehow or other, he meant to obtain a rifle. His father had a good one, and so had each of the acknowledged warriors of his band, but all the boys were as yet forced to put up with bows and arrows. Some of the braves even carried revolvers, and the hunting had been so poor that they were well supplied with ammunition. Two Arrows had learned from Sile that there were extra rifles and pistols, and no end of cartridges, in those wagons, but everybody knew that all that sort of thing had to be paid for, and Two Arrows lay awake a long time, feverishly wondering what he could find among those mountains to buy a rifle with, and a revolver and some ammunition. He felt that he should be a mere boy, after all, and not a full-grown brave, until he could exchange his bow and arrows for weapons which would kill a bear at long range. He wished never to have to wait for another on the top of any rock. It was the only point in which he could see that Sile had any real advantage over him to balance the humiliation of being a pale-face instead of the son of a Nez Percé chief. He was compelled to admit one more in the morning, for he had forgotten the fishing-rods and hooks and lines, and Sile was up before it was light, ready to begin his duty of keeping the camp supplied with provisions.

"We won't walk this time," he said, in a very business-like way. "We'll just ride across to the river and catch enough for breakfast and hurry back. None of the men can be spared from their work."

The sun arose very grandly over the magnificent mountain ranges, but he showed them all that wonderful scenery in vain. Sile was fishing for provisions for his father's men, and Two Arrows thought of rifles and pistols every time he pulled in a trout. He did not speak of the weight upon his mind as yet, but he was gradually forming a purpose of doing so at the earliest opportunity. It was almost like going to an open market for fish, except that there was nothing to pay for them. As fast as a line could be thrown, and its little silvery trap set a whirling, the hook was seized by some trout or other, large or small. Some of them were so heavy as to test the toughness of the upper joints of the rods, and now Two Arrows made a discovery. He had watched Sile work his reel until he had caught the secret of it, and could let a strong fish run a little before he drew him in. It was an idea that suited him exactly, and it made the fun more exciting.

"I say," exclaimed Sile, before a great while, "they're awful eaters, but they can't use up all we've got now. Let's just string 'em, and ride back to camp."

The movements of his hands, along with his words, explained his meaning, and Two Arrows pulled in his last fish with an "Ugh! good," for answer. He was doing one thing more rapidly than anybody had an idea of. He was a born "linguist," as many Indians are, and he was gathering words of English at a great rate. He was not sure he could yet utter correctly quite a number that he fully understood on hearing them, and his pride forbade him to make blunders. His trouble was with his tongue and not with his ears, as many an older fellow has found when he undertook to make a speech before critical people.

The camp was all astir when they rode in, and the coffee-pot was already upon the fire.

"That's the checker, my boy," said Yellow Pine, when he saw the fish. "We sha'n't do any starving. Let your horse feed a while, and then you and he go for some fresh meat. Look at *them!"*

There was a great grin upon his face as he pointed at Judge Parks and the miners. The judge had taken up a heavy hammer and was busily breaking masses of quartz to examine their quality, and the men had again gone at their building.

"Nary one of 'em's eaten a mouthful," said Pine, just as a chopper rested from his work to shout,

"We'll have enough shingles rived for the roof by the time them fellers gits their wall up;" and another said,

"Pine, that there clay-bank by the spring's the very best kind. It's most as good as mortar."

"'Tis if you temper it well," said Pine. "Call 'em to breakfast. There'll be fish br'iled and ready in no time."

Ha-ha-pah-no and Na-tee-kah each had a frying-pan, and the fish were put in as fast as they were cleaned, but some of the men could not wait for that. They insisted upon cleaning and cooking for themselves, for, as Jonas remarked,

"We can't git at the mine till the shelter's done and the waggins are unpacked. We'll have it up in short order."

As soon as he had finished his coffee and trout and "army bread," Sile went to take a look at what they were doing, and it made him open his eyes. The ground they had chosen, near a fine spring of water, was nearly level. They had marked out the lines of the walls they meant to build, and then along those lines they had dug a trench about a foot deep and two feet wide. No cellar was called for as yet, and the mason-work began at once. There was plenty of broken stone to be had, and it was rolled or carried with busy eagerness to the men who were laying the wall. One man at the clay-bank toiled zealously at the important task of mixing and tempering it, while another came and went with pailfuls that were used up as fast as he could bring them. The stones were laid with their smooth faces inward, and there was not a minute wasted in trimming anything for the sake of appearances. Sile could hardly believe that so much could have been done is so short a time, and he was again astonished when the men returned from breakfast. The wall grew at a tremendous rate. He went from that work to the place where the choppers were swinging their axes. A tall pine-tree, four feet in diameter at the base, was down shortly after the men went at it the previous evening, and now two sturdy fellows were making the chips fly as if they were chopping for a wager. They were evidently cutting the huge trunk into lengths of about three feet, and Sile was studying the matter when Two Arrows touched him on the elbow and pointed at the choppers.

"Ugh! What for?"

"Wait. Show him by-and-by," said Sile. "Make shingles to cover house."

"Ugh! Big lodge. Heap hard. No fall down. Top?"

"Yes. Make cover. Keep out rain."

"Ugh! Pale-face do a heap. Go away and leave him all," said Two Arrows.

It was the longest sentence he had yet attempted in English, and Sile looked at him with some surprise, but he should have remembered that Two Arrows had made a beginning long before that, and was but adding to it. At all events, he was correct in his conclusion that such a lodge could not be carried away, as could those for which Long Bear had sent his braves and squaws through the pass. It was perfectly certain that these would not loiter anywhere, but would go straight on their errand and return, and then the village would once more be under as good a shelter as it knew anything about or cared for.

All that day the axes fell, the wall grew fast, and Judge Parks and Yellow

Pine went on with their examinations and their other preparations for "opening the mine;" and all day long some other things went on without their knowing it.

Chapter XXIII

DANGER

The Apaches, in their encampment away down the river, cooked fish for breakfast at about the same hour that the miners did, but their trout had not been caught anything like so rapidly. It had required the work of several men, up and down the bank, for hours of the previous evening and for all the time since daylight, with their imperfect tackle, to get in enough for such a war-party. Nor had they cleaned or cooked so perfectly, and the fish had been eaten without pepper or salt. There was not a plate or a fork in the band, and there was not even a wish for coffee.

It was a hasty meal, greedily devoured, and then the marauders were once more in the saddle, or riding barebacked, as the case might be. All the while that the miners were so enthusiastically raising their stone lodge a peril they hardly thought of was pushing nearer and nearer. They knew well enough that they were in an Indian country, but were well assured that as yet no hostile red men could be aware of their arrival. It was also pretty sure that every stroke of work they did added to their security, for neither arrow nor bullet will go through a wall of quartz and granite two feet in thickness. Judge Parks had ideas of his own as to the future protection of the "notch," but the time had not yet come to say anything about them.

It was not many hours after the Apaches got in motion before they came to the forks of the stream, and here they halted for a general consultation. They already had well-mounted scouts ahead in both directions, and neither side had yet sent in any suggestion of danger discovered. They were evidently familiarly acquainted with the whole region, and there were arguments in favor of both lines of advance, but a gray-headed old warrior at last settled the question. He had been sitting quietly and listening to what others said until his turn seemed to come, but now he arose, and all seemed willing to listen. Pointing with his long, naked arm up the right fork of the river, he said, in his own harsh, gutteral tongue,

"Mountains. When blue-coats come, lose horses. Caught in big trap."

Turning and pointing up the other fork, he said,

"Morning. Hole in mountains. Blue-coats come. Go through hole. Get away. Come back some day, when blue-coats go home sick. Ugh!"

It was not a long speech, and it could hardly be described as "eloquent" but all the wiser and more influential braves said "Ugh!" and the road to the left was decided upon without any more discussion. That also decided in advance the course to be followed by Captain Grover and his cavalry, when they in their turn should reach the same point. Hour by hour they were slowly gaining upon the dangerous horse-thieves they were pursuing, and in due time they would surely learn whether or not they had a right to rejoice upon catching up with them. They were acting as the police and constables of a very disorderly community.

As for Long Bear and his Nez Percés, they had a very good reason for lazily hunting and fishing around their present camp until the return of the party which had gone for the hidden lodges, and so forth. Very few Indians need anything better than an excuse for not doing anything.

Two Arrows was not one of those Indians. Na-tee-kah continually called his attention to something new which she had discovered in the ways or in the possessions of those pale-faces. She was greatly interested in a curious wire "broiler." It opened, and a fish or a steak was put in, and it shut up and was put upon the coals, and when the cooking was finished, the long handles enabled you to take it off and not burn your fingers. There were twenty other things as wonderful as the broiler; and the judge had shown her how to wash her hands with soap, and had given her a pair of ear-rings and a silver buckle for her new blanket. She hardly knew what would come next, but she entirely sympathized with her brother in his own dream when he told her what it was.

"Ask pale-face chief," she said.

"Ugh! Laugh. Bow and arrows good enough for boy."

He said it almost bitterly, and Na-tee-kah stamped on the ground sharply as she responded,

"Two Arrows is a young chief. Big brave. Not a boy any more. Kill grisly. Kill cougar and big-horn. Bring back pony. Great chief in a little while. Give him rifle."

Two Arrows had a good enough opinion of himself, but he perfectly understood the easy good-nature with which he was treated by Yellow Pine and the rest. They regarded Sile as one bright boy and him as another, and had no idea of wasting costly rifles and such things upon him. He grew almost sullen over it, and was glad to get away from the camp when Sile came and asked him to go on a hunt with him.

This time there was a little pride as well as good-sense in his positive refusal to borrow a rifle. He was determined to shoot with his own weapons or none, and he rode away with no better ones than had been used by his tribe before they had ever heard of white men, and long before gunpowder had been invented. They were pretty good weapons yet, but there was one thing Two Arrows did not dream of. That was that it was not such a great number of years since the ancestors of these very pale-faces had gone to war and to hunt with bows and arrows vastly better than any ever carried by any red Indian in the world. The English race were bowmen once, just as they are riflemen now, shooting closer to the bull's-eye than any other.

Two Arrows felt that there was a sort of fever upon him. It made him hot and restless, and his eyes wandered searchingly in all directions, longing for an opportunity to do something which would bring him nearer to the prizes he coveted. Sile also was watching keenly the tops and branches of every clump of bushes they came to, but it almost seemed as if the game had suddenly migrated. It was natural that none should linger near the smoke and smell of camp-fires and cookery, but it was queer that the two young hunters should canter quietly on for mile after mile, and not so much as get a shot at a deer.

"We won't go back without something," said Sile. "I told father so. I mean to go right along. We can camp in the woods by ourselves if we don't kill anything early enough to get back to-night."

He had some trouble in making his meaning clear to Two Arrows, and the ambitious young Nez Percé was in precisely the frame of mind to agree with him. They even rode a little faster, and were hardly aware of the distance they had travelled. Sile was beginning to grow nervous about his reputation as a hunter and to remember that the camp had only a three days' supply of fresh meat, in spite of the fish. He believed that he had seen everything there was to be seen, but he was mistaken. Suddenly Two Arrows uttered a loud, astonished "Ugh!" sprang from his pony, and beckoned Sile to do the same, leading him hurriedly towards the nearest bushes.

Sile imitated his friend, without any idea of a reason for it, until Two Arrows took him by the arm and pointed away to the right towards the mountain range. They were on the crest of a high roll of ground, and could see for miles in some directions, except as the view was cut off by patches and strips of forest.

"Look! 'Pache!"

All that at first appeared to Sile's eyes were some moving black spots; but now he was able to show Two Arrows another of the advantages of a civilized man over a savage. Slung from his left shoulder was a small leathern case, and Two Arrows watched him closely while he opened it, took out something silver-mounted and handsome and put it to his eyes. Such things had been much discussed in his hearing, and he knew it was the "long eye of the pale-faces;" but he had no faith in it until Sile made him try it.

"There they are; six of 'em," said Sile. "Then look away down yonder and you'll see some more."

"No see us," said Two Arrows. "Come! Heap bad."

So it was, for the dreaded strangers were between them and the mountains. For all they knew, they might have ridden past others unseen, and these might intercept their return. Sile was only a white boy, and in an instant he understood that the young chief was the "captain" of their squad of two.

Two Arrows seemed to have the same notion instinctively, for anybody could read the look of blank uncertainty upon Sile's face. His binocular spy-glass could help him see farther and more accurately than the best pair of Indian eyes in the world, but it could not tell him what to do next.

"Come!" said Two Arrows, as he led his pony back down the slope and towards the forest that skirted the river. This was less than half a mile away, but the horses were not mounted until both were well under cover of it. It struck Sile that they might safely ride homeward along the stream, but Nez Percé training and caution forbade any such risk as that. Even the operation of reaching the bank might be full of peril, for nobody could guess at what moment they might stumble upon Apache warriors, and no others were at all likely to be there. It was most unlikely, however, that their enemies were advancing upon both sides of the water, and as soon as Two Arrows reached it he rode in. It was a wide and therefore shallow place, easily forded, and Sile breathed more freely as soon as he was under the shade of the woods beyond. His guide and captain pushed right on until they were out in a comparatively open reach of country, and then he turned to Sile, his whole face gleaming with uncontrollable excitement, and exclaimed,

"Ugh! Ride now. Kill hoss. Save pale-face. Save Nez Percé. Get there before Apache. All scalp gone if 'Pache come first."

He suppressed a whoop, but the next bound of his pony explained his meaning, and Sile galloped, stride by stride, with him. It was a race for life and for the lives of many others; for Two Arrows had briefly read that problem when he said to Sile, as he handed him back his glass,

"No squaw. Braves on war-path. No hunt. Kill. Take scalp."

Both were well mounted, and Sile rode well, although by no means so completely at home on horseback as was his red friend. His rifle, too, was more tiresome to carry than was a light lance, and the bow and arrows were now tightly "slung," and required no handling. It would not do to wear out their horses in one rush, but they kept on at the highest speed at all consistent with a long ride. It was much faster, at all events, than the Apaches were likely to travel, unless something new should stir them up. By keeping well away from the stream, they were not compelled to follow its windings, and could ride more nearly in a straight line, only turning out for clumps of trees and similar obstructions and paying no attention to game, although they now saw gang after gang of deer and a respectable party of bisons.

Chapter XXIV

SILE'S VICTORY

There had been no anxiety at the mine on account of the absent hunters. Judge Parks and Yellow Pine had their hands very full of an inspection of the cargoes of the two wagons. The men toiled vigorously at the stone wall and at the shingle riving. Ha-ha-pah-no and Na-tee-kah were as busy as bees over the lengthening list of marvels put before their eyes. It seemed to Na-tee-kah as if Judge Parks must be a kind of magician, or else that he had a whole lodge full of "medicine-men" of a rare breed at home, who could conjure up for him almost anything he might chose to call for. It was no use to try to understand such things as he and Yellow Pine were examining. They belonged to the great mystery of pale-face life, and a Nez Percé girl could not be expected to guess very nearly at their uses. She could comb her hair more carefully, however, and discover a new way of doing it up, and she did not know how closely she was imitating many pale-face young ladies of about her age, not to speak of older ones.

Noon came and went, and there were no signs of returning hunters or of game of any sort, but there was no danger of famine in that camp for days and days to come.

Judge Parks would hardly have unpacked mining-tools and "fixings," as Pine called them, so composedly if he could have known what was going forward farther down the valley and on the other side of the little river.

On, on rode Two Arrows and his companion, and it almost seemed as if both were growing older. It was no sort of boy-play to ride like that, with such tremendous consequences depending upon them. Sile's merry face put on a tremendously sober and earnest expression, while Two Arrows looked as if he were already a chief in command of a war-party. So he was, only that the party was a very small one.

Mile after mile went by, and the horses held out capitally; but at last Two Arrows slackened his gait, seemed to make a silent calculation, and halted.

"Pale-face camp there," he said, emphatically, pointing across towards the mountain range at their left. "Red-head cross water. Tell his people. Two Arrows ride. Tell Nez Percé. Red-head go straight, find camp. Ugh!"

"I can find it," said Sile. "I was thinking we'd gone up river about far enough. We must have got away ahead of the Apaches. Hope I sha'n't meet any."

"Shoot quick," said Two Arrows. "Kill. Take 'calp. Be great brave. Two Arrows kill grisly. Kill 'Pache some day. How!"

He held out his hand, and Sile shook it hard in token of good-bye, and the two boys separated, each to carry his own tidings and face his own dangers. Two Arrows rode on in a straight line up the valley, and Sile wheeled towards the line of forest which bordered the river. It struck him that he was yet a little below the precise neighborhood of the mine, and he was correct, but as yet it was all guess-work. At all events, he was sure that his remaining ride could not be a long one; it could not fail to be intensely exciting. Again he saw plenty of game, and he was strangely tempted to try a shot at a deer until the idea came to him,

"I can't say what ears might hear the report of my rifle."

Deer did not seem to be of any account after that idea took form, and he galloped on. In a few minutes more his horse's feet were in the water, and he was almost immediately aware that he had not chosen a good ford. It grew deep too fast, and he had to ride out again.

"I won't go into another pool," he said to himself. "I'll hunt for a wide place where it ripples well."

He had not the experience and the quick eyes of Two Arrows, but he was learning fast, and it was easy to find a better crossing. Once over, he felt that the forest was itself a sort of protection, and there came a great thrill all over him at the thought of riding out from under it. What if the Apaches should be already there, and what if they had found the camp and destroyed it?

"They haven't done that," said Sile, "unless they managed to take it by surprise. Guess they couldn't do that in broad daylight. Our men are all old hands, and Yellow Pine keeps his eyes about him. I'll get in a good while before dark—that is, if I make out to get in. I wish there was good cover all the way."

He drew rein for a moment under the last line of trees, and he looked earnestly in all directions, but even his spy-glass could not reveal to him a sign of danger. He had never seen anything more absolutely quiet and peaceful than was that stretch of open valley, with its grass and its bushes, and its clusters of grand old trees. It encouraged him a good deal to see a buck and two does feeding within a quarter of a mile of him, and he at once rode watchfully onward. His horse was beginning to show signs of hard riding, and he noted it regretfully. There might yet be a race to run, for all he knew.

There was to be something very different from a race, and the notice of it came to him very suddenly. Just as he rode out through a patch of willows in a long hollow, walking his horse because of their being in his way a little, his heart seemed to stop beating and stand still. Then it beat again, and like a trip-hammer, for a moment. The bridle fell from his hand, and he made ready his rifle as if by an instinctive movement.

Right before him and hardly a hundred yards away, on the rising ground, sat an Indian brave, in his war-paint, upon a very fine looking horse, and Sile was sure at a glance that he could not be one of his Nez Percé friends. They had no such horses as that among all that he and Two Arrows had found for them. The warrior was looking in the opposite direction at the instant, but he was also wheeling his horse, and in a second or so more he caught sight of Sile. He had a lance, but it was slung behind him, and in his hands was as good a repeating-rifle as Sile's own, and he raised it like a flash.

It was as if he lifted two, for Sile's rifle also came up with precisely the same quick, ready-handed motion.

It was an awful moment for Sile. He had never before done as much real thinking in one hour as he did between his first glimpse of that redskin and the rising of the dark, threatening line of that rifle-barrel.

He had thought of the men at the mine, and of their need of warning, and therefore of the necessity that he should protect himself and get to them alive. He had thought of his father and his mother, and of some other people, and he had also thought what a dreadful thing it was to shoot straight at a man, and perhaps to kill him. He had just said to himself,

"I might just kill his horse, and then I could get away from him."

At that very instant the two rifles came to a level, whether he would or not. He felt no symptoms of "buck ague" this time, for every nerve and muscle of his body was stiffening, while his tired horse stood as still as a stone. That was where he had a priceless advantage. The spirited animal ridden by his enemy was a trifle restive for some reason, and caused a shade of delay that was just enough to give Sile his only remaining chance.

"If I hit his horse in the head," he was thinking as he pulled the trigger: but that would have been close shooting at a hundred yards, and just beyond the head of the horse was the naked breast of the warrior.

There were two reports close together, and Sile felt something prick him sharply on the left arm near the shoulder. At the same moment he saw the red man reel to and fro upon his horse, and then pitch off head foremost into the grass.

"Oh, dear me, I've shot him!" he exclaimed, and his first impulse was to ride away as fast as he could.

Then came a suggestion that the brave might be only wounded, and that it was his duty to go and see if he could do anything for him. With that, too, there came a great gush of curiosity and a fierce and feverish sense of triumph. He had fought a duel on horseback with an Indian warrior, with rifles, and there were no other white boys who could say that they had done that. He sat still upon his horse for a moment, and his breath came and went very quickly, and then he somewhat cautiously rode forward. The Indian's horse had bounded away for a little distance when his master fell, but was now standing and looking at him, as if in doubt as to what he ought to do next. Not another human being of any kind was to be seen, but Sile looked around him anxiously enough to make sure that he was alone. Not one sound disturbed the peaceful silence of the valley after those two rifles had spoken.

All irresolution passed out of Sile's mind as he rode forward, for he felt that he had behaved rightly, and had done nothing for which he could blame himself. He watched the fallen man narrowly as he drew near him, but there was no motion or any other sign of life.

"I must have killed him outright!" He sprang from his horse and bent over the prostrate form, but he did not have to look more than once. "That hole— that's where the bullet went in. It must have gone right through his heart. Well, he would have killed me if I had not killed him. I would not have hurt him if I could have helped it."

It seemed to Sile a matter of course that he should pick up the red warrior's rifle, unbuckle and take off the bead-worked belt that carried his knife and revolver, take his lance, catch his horse, and then ride onward, carrying with him all as "spoils of war." He did it coolly and steadily but rapidly, and without any idea how very fast he was growing. He was learning lessons in a great school, but any wise old man could have told him that no two boys learn the same lessons anywhere. A good deal more depends upon the boy himself than upon the school or the teacher.

That tall, brawny Apache warrior had been a distinguished brave, and he had been sent upon a scouting trip away in advance of the rest merely as a customary precaution. There had been no expectation that he would discover anything remarkable. In meeting a solitary pale-face, he had undertaken to kill him very much as a matter of course, for he was just then at war with all white men. Sile had made the better shot of the two, and that was about all that could be said. As for Sile, he was in a greater hurry than ever to get to the mine, and again and again he wondered whether Two Arrows had met any Apaches.

"I do hope he hasn't," he said to himself, "with only a bow and arrows. I wish he had a rifle."

Chapter XXV

A MIDNIGHT MARCH

When Two Arrows parted from Sile he was well aware that the errand of the Red-head had more real peril in it than his own, and he would not have had him armed with only a bow and arrows; but oh how he did long for a repeating-rifle for his own use! He had been hungry enough for one before; but now that there was a promise of war it seemed to him that the only thing in the world worth the having, except a horse, was one of the white man's terrible weapons. With such as he now had he had killed wild animals and won for himself a name and fame, but in spite of that he almost despised them. What could he do now, for instance, against an Apache well armed, as all that warlike tribe were said to be?

He also had a prejudiced idea that if Sile were to meet one of them he would be in a manner helpless—a mere ignorant, green, untaught, unready, white boy, not the son of a Nez Percé chief, nor skilled in the wiles and ways of Western warfare. As for himself, he felt quite confident that all he needed wherewith to meet and overcome anything or anybody was just such a perfect "repeater" as Sile carried. He somehow overlooked the fact that he had never practised much with one, while Sile belonged to the race that made them. He had been used to a bow and arrows from the time he had learned to ride, and almost from the time he had learned to walk; so that, after all, they might be his safest weapon.

He rode on steadily for a few miles, and then he crossed the stream and proceeded under cover of the trees. It was time to travel more slowly, for his pony had no gallop left in him. The approach to the camp even was made with some caution, but there was no need of any.

The sun was going down, and the fires were blazing brightly. The hunters had done well that day, and there were preparations for much eating. Two Arrows knew at a glance that all things were working prosperously, and that his people had no suspicion of any danger near them. The vast importance of his errand filled him very full, and he halted under the shadow of the trees.

Warriors were stalking around here and there, or were lazily stretched upon the ground. Squaws were busily dressing skins, or cooking or chattering with one another, and children were hungrily watching the cookery and wishing that their turns to be fed might come pretty soon. Old One-eye was at work upon a well-covered bone before going out for his usual night-watch and patrol, but he was suddenly called upon to drop it and to raise his head for a howl.

Out of the growing darkness in the edge of the woods there came a quick series of sharp, threatening, warning whoops, uttered in a shrill and youthful voice that the dog knew perfectly. So did others, for Long Bear sprang to his feet, exclaiming,

"Ugh! Two Arrows!" and answered him with a whoop of such volume and meaning that every brave and boy who heard it understood it as a command, and ran for his weapons first, and then to the corral to see about his pony.

Two Arrows dismounted and led his over-ridden pony into camp. Long Bear stood silently and dignifiedly in front of his lodge waiting for him, and the older warriors were gathering fast to hear the news. They knew very well that no Indian boy would have dared to give such a signal as that without good reason, and their faces were clouding seriously.

"Two Arrows speak quick," said his father. "All hear him."

The young scout felt deeply the pride of his position. He pointed towards the lower valley with all the dignity he could muster, and uttered only the words,

"'Pache! War-path!"

There was a dismal chorus of "Ugh!" from all who heard him, but there was not one war-whoop. He was at once called upon for a minute and careful account of the whole affair, including the locality and condition of Judge Parks and his party of miners. He made his report with a fullness and keenness of observation that stirred up the old chief's family pride amazingly.

"Young chief," he remarked. "Do something more every time."

It looked very much like it, and his return as an intelligent and successful scout added largely to all his other claims to distinction. Not another boy in the band had ever announced anything so very bad and so important.

That was no time for anybody to spend a thought upon the fame of Two Arrows, however. All the old men said, one after another, that they wished they knew just how many Apaches there were in that war-party. Had they known how very strong it was, they might have been even worse puzzled, but Long Bear was really a clear-headed leader, and he decided the whole matter promptly and finally. He told his gathering braves that the place where they were was a bad one to fight in, while their pale-face friends had selected a peculiarly good one. They themselves had but twenty-three warriors armed with rifles, and nearly as many more young men and well-grown boys armed with bows and arrows. That was no force with which to meet Apaches, nobody knew how many, and all sure to be riflemen. To go back through the pass was to die of sure starvation, even if they were not followed and slaughtered among the rocks. The Apaches were plainly making for that very pass, he said; and he was only a keen-eyed chief and not at all a prophet when he read the matter correctly and said,

"'Pache run away from blue-coats. All in a hurry. Not stop. Nez Percé hide and let them go by. Not fight. Keep pony. Keep hair. Good. Ugh!"

The party which had been sent back after the lodges and things was a serious anxiety, and a light-footed youngster was started off at once to warn them. He would be sure to meet them on their way, returning, and could tell them to be on their guard, and very little more could be done for them.

Long Bear finished his speech of explanation, and then, without a moment's pause, he gave the order to break up camp and prepare to march, carrying with them every pound of provisions. Not one moment was to be lost in gaining such protection as might be had from the good position of the miners, and from the fact that they were pale-faces of some importance, and from the other great fact that they were all good riflemen. There was hardly anybody in the band, old enough to understand what an Apache was, who did not fully appreciate the force of the chief's argument, and every squaw did her best to hasten the departure. Lodges came down, ponies were packed, children were gathered, warriors and braves and boys completed their preparations for fighting; the Big Tongue declared his readiness to kill a large number of Apaches, and One-eye was compelled to abandon forever all the bones he had buried since the people he barked for had settled upon the bank of that river.

There was a good deal of quiet and sober efficiency in spite of the excitement. Two Arrows had further questions to answer from quite a number of his elders. He was furnished with one of the best ponies in the drove in acknowledgment of his services. He was now, also, to figure as a kind of guide, and he did not once think of or mention the fatigue of his long, hard ride. He very willingly ate, however, the whole of a buffalo steak, broiled for him by one of the squaws, and felt a good deal better afterwards. He almost felt that he had earned a rifle, or at least a pistol, but well knew that it was all in vain to ask for one, when the supply was insufficient to arm all the braves who were a full head taller than himself.

Still, it was a magnificent thing, at last, to ride out at the head of the cavalcade, by the side of a tall warrior, as the one boy of all that band who was on first-rate terms with the pale-faces and knew perfectly the trail leading to them. As for that, any red man of them all could have followed the tracks of the wagon-wheels, even at night, but Two Arrows had no idea of surrendering that part of his growing importance. It would have done Na-tee-kah's proud heart good to have seen him in particular, and it would have been well worth the while of almost anybody else to have had a good look at the whole affair, as the motley array poured out into the moonlight from under the shadowy cover of the primeval forest.

There were no sleepy ones except the pappooses, and they could sleep under the tightly-drawn blankets upon the backs of their mothers as well as anywhere else. All the rest were more or less hardened to the quick changes and migrations of the kind of life into which they had been born. They were not likely to be injured by being kept up pretty late for one night, and there was no need that anybody should walk, now that their four-footed wealth had returned.

Two Arrows thought of that, and he could hardly help reminding some of his friends of his share in so good a thing. He received a reply from one gray-headed warrior which sounded very much like a snub:

"Ugh! Two Arrows. Red-head. Boys find pony first. Pony there. Brave find next day. Boy talk too much. Kill 'Pache like warrior. Then talk a heap. Show scalp. Whoop. Ugh!"

As for war and that sort of thing, there was no need for anybody to stir the ambition of Two Arrows up to a greater heat. He was ready enough now to do the wildest and rashest things he could think of. He felt as if he were out upon his first war-path, and that there must be somewhere a great heap of glory preparing for him.

The Nez Percé camp had been broken up with great celerity, and no time had been lost, but after all the summons to move had come upon them most unexpectedly. There had been a great deal to do and but a dim light to do it by, and so it was pretty late before the picturesque caravan was in motion. It took a line of march towards the mountains until its head struck the well-marked tracks of the loaded wagons, and from that point forward its course required little guiding. By a stern command from Long Bear the utmost silence was maintained, and, after the moon went down, the movement might fairly be said to have been performed in secret. There was no danger that any small squad of Apache scouts would assail so strong a party. Even the squaws and children felt pretty safe, but it was very hard upon the Big Tongue, for that great brave soon found himself in an advanced party, commanded by Long Bear himself, and after that he was under an absolute necessity of not saying anything.

THE MOONLIGHT MARCH OF NEZ PERCÉSToList

Chapter XXVI
PREPARING FOR AN ATTACK

A good while before Two Arrows reached the camp of his people Judge Parks and Yellow Pine discovered that they had done about as much as they could at the mouth of what was yet to be the mine until they should have men to help them. The judge handed to Na-tee-kah another book of pictures to wonder over, and then he and Pine went upon a tour of inspection. They found the choppers busy with beetles and wedges upon the lengths of easily-cloven pine, and the heap of long, wide slabs or shingles for the roof was growing rapidly.

"We can make it weather-tight with moss-packing," said Pine, "and if we can't have sash and glass we can make good solid doors and shutters."

"There will be storms," said the judge.

"Yes, but the winters are never hard down here. Even if we got snowed in it wouldn't stay long, and the supply-train'll get here before the end of next month. Can't lose its way."

"I should say not. But now just look at that wall."

It was worth looking at, if only for the way in which it was rising. The mud and stones went into place with a perfect rush. At that rate there would quickly be a finished house there, such as it was to be. All was well and solidly laid, too, and the inner face was smooth enough. That was more than could be said for the outside, and Pine remarked,

"Reckon nobody'll care to rub himself very hard against the side of that shelter when it's done."

From the house they both strolled away for a look at the animals, and then on down to the mouth of the notch. They were noting with care the several peculiarities of the rocky elevations to the right and left, when the judge felt his arm gripped very hard, and Yellow Pine exclaimed,

"Look there, jedge! Something's happened to the young redskin."

Judge Parks carried a spy-glass as good as Sile's and it was up instantly. "That's Sile, but the horse he's leading isn't a pony. Look, Pine."

"I'd call it—How close this thing does bring 'em. I could count his buttons. He's carrying two rifles and a lance. Something mighty queer has turned up, jedge, but you can see that Sile's all right. What can have become of Two

Arrows? I hope he hasn't been wiped out. He was the likeliest kind of a young chap."

"We'll know when he gets here."

Waiting was about all they could do, but they grew more and more impatient until Sile came within hail. After that the questions and answers chased each other back and forth until the entire account of Sile's hunt and its ending was perfectly understood.

Sile saw his father shudder and turn pale, and then flush fiery red, while he described his encounter with the Apache. He had dismounted before he got to that, and the next thing he felt was a pair of arms around him, and he heard Yellow Pine exclaim,

"I could a'most hug the young rooster myself. It was jest the gamest kind of thing to do. I say, Sile, he barked ye on yer left arm. I'd call it, now, if that there wasn't close work. Take yer jacket off."

Sile had hardly paid any attention to that matter, although his arm had felt a little stiff, and there was really not much of a hurt. In another instant his father was saying so, but he said it with a peculiar look upon his face. The Indian's bullet had been a "Minie-ball," of course, and, as it grazed his arm, one of its ragged edges had torn through the cloth and touched the flesh only just enough to break the skin and draw a little blood. Sile could fairly say he was "wounded," and no more, and Yellow Pine remarked,

"Reckon we won't send ye to the hospital for that; but I'm all-fired glad it didn't go any nigher. It's jest on a line to where it would ha' knocked yer arm off, if it had struck onto the bone. It's the narrerest kind of an escape."

Judge Parks had nothing more to say, for some reason, and seemed willing that Sile should go right on with further particulars of the day.

"Two Arrows is right," said Pine. "He'd know a war-party, sure. It's war with us, anyhow, and there isn't but one thing to be done. The men must knock off from the house, and come right down and block this 'ere opening with logs and rocks. We can make the best kind of a rifle-pit. Only leave room for one man, or for one hoss at a time, to get in or out."

"That's it," said the judge. "Now, Sile, come along. You must let the men see what you've been up to. They'll know exactly what it means."

Sile had a curious sense of bashfulness about it, but he followed his father, and in a few minutes more the rough, bearded, red-shirted fellows were giving him three of the most ringing cheers he had ever heard. Ha-ha-pah-no and Na-tee-kah looked at him with something that was half wonder. They could not have believed it, but for the horse and the lance, and the rifle and the belt. Here was the Red-head, a mere pale-face boy, bringing in trophies of which a great warrior might have been proud. Na-tee-kah had a sort of notion that Two Arrows must have done it somehow, until well assured that her brother had not been present, and that the Red-head had not taken the scalp of the slain Apache. She had heard that the pale-face warriors sometimes neglected that duty, but could not well understand why, even when Ha-ha-pah-no explained to her that it was "bad medicine" for a white man to scalp anybody.

The situation called for something more than cheers, however, and the miners hurried to the mouth of the notch. To pack it breast-high with fragments of wood and stone was no great matter, and the breastwork was finished in time for a late supper.

"Tell ye what, jedge," remarked one of the men, "if I was a redskin I wouldn't be in a hurry to ride up to that there bar, with a half a dozen rifles peepin' over it. Reckon it'd take the cleanest kind of grit. A feller could stand behind it and pepper away, and be a'most safe agin anything short of cannon."

The wagons and other things were left as they were, and the entire notch was a perfectly safe corral for the animals. All the human beings moved their bivouac down towards the barrier they had made, leaving the fires behind them.

"They're all right, there," said Pine, "and we needn't kindle any down hereaway to tell jest where we are."

There was sense in that, and one sentry was as good as a dozen to keep watch at the narrow entrance left, for even that was securely closed until there should be a good reason for opening it.

Sile found himself the hero of the camp, and that the scratch upon his arm excused him from guard duty. At first he was well pleased to lie down and go to sleep, after the severe fatigue and excitement of his great ride. Never before had he raced it after such a fashion, and every bone and muscle felt the effects of the long strain. He saw, too, that everybody else was taking the matter with perfect coolness. All those miners had been in tight places more than once, and they had great faith in the prudence of redskins about charging upon white riflemen hidden behind rocks. Sile ate a hearty supper. In fact, he was compelled at last to be very positive with Ha-ha-pah-no. She would have gone right on cooking for him until morning if he had let her, and so would Na-tee-kah. They were positively proud of the privilege of bringing him his coffee. He was assured that the horse and weapons of the Apache warrior were his own personal property, and he examined them again and again with a sense of ownership that he had never felt for anything else. He could not tell why, until Jonas remarked to him,

"If you hadn't pulled straight, your plunder'd be in the 'Pache camp 'bout now, scalp and all. It was jest a question of grit and shootin'. I'm powerful glad you made out to throw yer lead to the right spot."

So was Sile, but it was not easy, somehow, for him to make up his mind that he had really killed anybody. He found a queer idea in his mind several times that before long that Apache warrior would wake up and wonder what had become of his horse and his weapons. Not long after supper he curled up in his blanket at the foot of a tree, and in a few minutes he was soundly asleep. He did not hear his father say to Yellow Pine, as the two bent over him,

"My brave boy!"

Nor did he hear Pine grumble,

"If he hasn't earned a good snooze, then nobody has. Tell ye what, jedge, that feller'll be guv'ner of a State one of these days. I'd vote for him. I'd like to have seen him 'changing shots with that there redskin."

They moved away, and the judge remarked,

"We are safe enough for to-night, but they'll find us to-morrow."

"Maybe, maybe not. I can't quite make it out as to what could bring 'em away up here. Two Arrows told Sile they was a war-party, and if that's so, they must have been licked somewhere. They'd never have cut it for these ranges without somebody was after 'em."

"Perhaps so. We'll see. Anyhow, we can keep a sharp lookout."

There was no danger that any sentry would sleep on his post that night, but all the first part and the middle of it went by as peacefully as if the valley were uninhabited.

Sile slept and slept, and when at last he opened his eyes, he could not have told why he did so. The stars were shining. The night air was crisp and chilly, but he was warm under his blanket. It took him almost a minute to gather his thoughts and understand where he really was. That was partly because he had been sleeping heavily, and partly because, at the very last, he had dreamed of being at home, and of leading a remarkable horse into the sitting-room to show it to his mother.

It was a strange place to wake up in, and he could dimly see the forms of other men, rolled in blankets, lying near, each with a rifle lying by him ready for prompt use.

"They won't be taken by surprise," said Sile to himself. "I'm going down for a look at the barrier. I've lain still long enough."

He felt a little stiff when he first rose to his feet, but it passed away when he stretched himself and began to walk. His left arm pained him more than he had expected, and he found it slightly swollen. It was not precisely like the same scratch made in any other way, and he was glad that there was no more of it. Still, he hardly knew what he had that he valued more highly than that light hurt upon his arm. It had made a sort of soldier of him. It was a promotion, and he vaguely hoped that it would leave a scar. Then he half wished that the scar might come out upon his face, where it would not be forever covered up by his coat-sleeve.

"My new horse is in the corral, and I couldn't pick him out now. My lance and things are in the wagon. I'll go and have a look at the barrier. I'm feeling tip-top."

CHAPTER XXVII

FROM BOW TO RIFLE

Leaning over the upper log of the barrier, rifle in hand, and peering out upon the starlit slope beyond him, stood the form of Jonas, the miner. Not a sound came to him from the mists and shadows of the valley, and he was just remarking, aloud,

"It's as quiet as a cornfield," when a voice at his elbow explained,

"Hist! Ha-ha-pah-no—sh-sh!" and Na-tee-kah dropped upon the ground, and pressed her little round ear against it. So, almost instantly, did Ha-ha-pah-no, and he heard Sile saying,

"Their ears are better than yours or mine if they can hear anything."

"Didn't know there was one of ye nigh me," said Jonas. "That's the way for a feller to lose his hair—looking too hard in one direction while somebody comes up behind him. No, Sile, I haven't heerd a thing."

Na-tee-kah sprang to her feet.

"Horse come. Ugh!" and she held up her hand for silence, while Ha-ha-pah-no also arose, listening intently.

"Indian ears for it," said Jonas. "'Pears to me I can hear something now myself."

"I can't, then," said another voice. It was that of a sleepy miner, who had waked up to follow Sile, just as he had been awakened by even the noiseless movements of the squaws.

"Hark!" exclaimed Jonas.

It was the sound of galloping, and then a shrill whoop.

"Two Arrows!" screamed Na-tee-kah. "'Pache get him!"

Jonas had already thrown down the logs of wood in the opening, and now he shouted,

"Rifles, boys! Ready!"

There was a great shout from the bivouac behind them, but it seemed almost no time before a pony and his rider dashed into dim view before them, followed by a larger shadow, from which came whoop after whoop.

"Take the hind one. Give it to him," shouted Jonas, as a streak of fire sprang from his own rifle-muzzle. Two other shots followed, as if there were any chance of hitting a galloping horseman in such a half darkness as that. Hit or no hit, one Apache warrior was so utterly astounded that he drew rein, all but throwing his horse upon his haunches, and the pony rider he was pursuing wheeled sharply to the right. Half a minute later and all would have been over with Two Arrows, in all probability, but, as matters had now turned, it was his enemy who had made a blunder. He sat for several precious seconds almost motionless, although not a shot had touched him, and by so doing he put himself up for a target at very short arrow range. The next instant he was dashing wildly away into the darkness, for the horse had an arrow in his flank to spur him, and the brave himself had a similar token of the skill of Two Arrows projecting from his right thigh.

"Sile," said Jonas, "he got it. You can tell that by the yell he gave."

"Come on in," shouted Sile. "There may be more of 'em. We're all up and ready for 'em."

It looked like it, as man after man came hurrying forward, but Two Arrows quieted them on that head. He had been sent forward by Long Bear to announce the coming of the Nez Percés, and he had encountered the Apache less than half a mile from the notch. It had been a close race, although he had a fresh pony and a good start. Any hurt to his pride on account of arriving in that precise manner, followed instead of following, was more than cured by the undoubted fact that he had sent an arrow into his pursuer.

"There wasn't really any show for bullet-work," said Jonas, "but lead'll hurt jest as bad in the dark, in case it gits there."

"All come," said Na-tee-kah. "Good. Two Arrows great brave now. Strike warrior. Fight a heap."

Judge Parks was not sorry to hear of such an addition to his little garrison, as the Nez Percé warriors could be fully depended upon to fight well for their ponies and lives. It was not a great while before the head of their cavalcade came out of the shadows, and deeper and more sonorous whoops answered that of Two Arrows.

"Big Tongue," said Ha-ha-pah-no. "Heap mouth!"

There surely was one whoop that seemed to have swallowed several others, and Jonas remarked,

"That feller could do all the loose yelling for a small tribe. Hark to him, now."

"Big Tongue great brave!" said Ha-ha-pah-no, tartly. "'Pache hear him,

'Pache go dead. Run."

In a few minutes more the Nez Percé ponies were squeezing their packs through the narrow entrance of the notch, and a succession of approving grunts from Long Bear testified the satisfaction he felt at getting into so secure a fort. He perfectly understood the value and uses of that barrier. When daylight came he again said "Ugh!" several times while he was examining the stone wall and the other evidences of the skill and zeal of his pale-face friends.

There was no more sleeping done in the notch, but there was an immense amount of very early cooking and eating, not to speak of the smoking and consultation, and the very general expression of a bad opinion of the entire Apache nation. They and their works, past, present, and to come, were condemned unsparingly. At the same time their fighting qualities were freely admitted, and with them the certainty that no Apache war-party would turn away from a bit of war so well begun as was this.

The sun arose, but almost to the astonishment of Sile, as well as the Nez Percés, the hardy miners behaved very much as if they had no war whatever on their hands.

"Them 'Paches'll come and go," said Jonas, "but we've got to have this 'ere wall finished."

At it they went, well assured that the barrier and all the land near it would be well watched, and that it was an easy thing to do to pick up a rifle if an alarm should come.

Sile felt less interest in the mine, somehow. The story of his exploit had been told, of course, to his Indian friends, and he could but see that it had made him an object of respectful admiration. There was not a warrior among them who would not have been proud of such a feather as that victory, but the effect upon Two Arrows was peculiar. He had regarded himself as Sile's superior in all things which did not belong especially to a young pale-face. It had not occurred to him that Sile was or ever could become a "great brave." Some of the "blue-coats" were, he knew, but Sile was not a blue-coat. He had heard stories of the prowess of other pale-faces, but Sile was a mere boy, and dreadfully green to the ways of the plains and mountains. He could not think of one boy of his band who really knew less of the things most important to be known, except rifle-shooting. His pride was touched in a tender spot, for although he was sure he had sent an arrow into an Apache, he had nothing to show for it. Na-tee-kah was enormously proud of that arrow, and Ha-ha-pah-no was compelled to remind her that her hero brother had brought in neither scalp nor horse, and had saved his own by the timely rifle practice of Sile and the men at the gap. For all that, Na-tee-kah had a vivid persuasion that, if the pale-faces had not interfered and driven away the Apache, there would have been more glory earned by the young chief of the Nez Percés. She could not be dissatisfied with Sile, however. After a brief consultation with his father, the Red-head went to the wagon and brought out the rifle he had won and with it a box of cartridges. It was a capital weapon, in good condition, and Sile showed it to Two Arrows with a great glow on his face and with a sense of standing up uncommonly straight. Several braves gathered to look at it and to declare it "heap good gun."

Two Arrows held it for a moment, with a look which did not need any interpreter. It was intensely wistful, and had a quick flash of keen jealousy in it. What was there that he could not do with such a splendid tool of destruction as that, instead of his lance and bow? He was nothing but a poor red youngster, after all, compelled to wait, he could not guess how long, before he could hope to be armed as a complete brave. He held out the rifle to Sile dejectedly, but then something like a shiver went all over him, for Sile only pushed it back, saying,

"No; Two Arrows keep it. Take present. Good friend." And then he held out the little waterproof box of copper cartridges of the size called for by that rifle.

Two Arrows required a breath or so before he could believe that the thing was a reality, and then he broke out into a yell of delight.

One-eye, standing behind him, began to bark vociferously, although nobody had given him anything except unlimited bones.

Every Nez Percé brave present deemed it his duty to shake hands with Sile, and Long Bear was summoned at once to do the same. Two Arrows found himself terribly short of words to tell how he felt about it, but he flatly refused to make a trial of that gun then and there. He felt such a dancing in his head and in his fingers that he was hardly sure he could hit the side of the mountain, and he did not care to disgrace his marksmanship before so many crack shots. It even occurred to him that he was not likely to come out of a duel on horseback as well as Sile until he should have had some practice. He did not know how steadily Sile had insisted on trying several shots every day since the mining expedition started. At all events he had mounted one round more in the ladder of his ambition, and had a better prospect for the next.

Chapter XXVIII
THE APACHES HAVE COME

Just as the sun was rising that morning, an altogether used-up horse came staggering into the awaking camp of the Apache war-party. On the horse was a warrior who had been sent out, with others, on scouting duty the previous day, and he now seemed nearly as fatigued as did the animal he rode. He had strength for a whoop whose meaning startled all who heard it, and in a minute more it was understood by most of them that the horse had been so badly tired out by one arrow, and the brave by another; but they did not know of whom they were speaking when they gruffly remarked,

"Two Arrows. Ugh! Nez Percé."

The baffled scout was unable to testify to the presence of white men, although he could aver that he had retreated from several busy rifles. He had deemed it his duty to ride back with his news and for another horse. It would be a good while before he could do much walking, and the horse which had carried him in must be abandoned, whether it should live or die.

There was nothing to dispirit such a company in the prospect of more plunder, many ponies and scalps, and an easy victory over a hunting party trespassing upon their acknowledged range. They did but eat breakfast more rapidly and push forward at once. The idea was yet strong upon them that they were pursued, but not one of their rearward scouts had come in, and a sense of false security had begun to creep over all but the very grayest heads among them. Even of these not one dreamed how dangerously near was the steady advance of Captain Grover and his blue-coats.

It is an old proverb of sea-fighting that "a stern chase is a long chase," and it is nearly as true on land, but the cavalry had pushed along with steady persistency, in a thoroughly business-like and scientific economy of time and horses. They were therefore in pretty good condition, men and animals. As Captain Grover remarked so it had been:

"I know about how fast the redskins can travel. They stole a whole grist of slow stock and that measures their gait."

However swift might be their best, the Apaches had gone no farther any day than the slowest half-dozen of their plunder. Captain Grover was therefore almost justified in a firm conviction he expressed that morning:

"Now for it, boys. We shall be among 'em before sunset."

On pushed the cavalry with enthusiasm, but at the same hour the Apaches were also pressing forward with increasing eagerness. They were no longer in one body. All their drove of stolen quadrupeds and their own superfluous ponies made up a sort of rear-guard, driven and cared for by about a dozen of the less distinguished braves, with orders to make as good speed as possible. The remainder of the force, full of whooping and yelling and a great hunger for glory and ponies, rode forward to find the Nez Percés. It could not be hard to do that, with so clear an idea as to the locality of at least several of them, but there was a surprise ready.

They had hardly ridden an hour when the foremost warriors made the air ring with whoops of wrath, and in a moment more the word "pale-face" was passing from rider to rider. They had found the victim of Sile's marksmanship, and the fact that he had not been scalped put away the idea that he had fallen before a Nez Percé. The trail of the two horses leading away to the left was plainly marked and could be followed, and there was no reason for special caution in so open a country. Still, the onward movement from that point was made in a more compact body and in something like silence. The trail before them led in the precise direction indicated by the brave shot by Sile, and the presence of both Nez Percés and pale-faces in that valley was of itself a sort of enigma. Word was left for the rear-guard to halt at the spot where the body lay until rejoined by the main force.

The garrison at the notch was ignorant of all this, but while the house-builders toiled at their wall with undiminished energy Long Bear sent out several of his best braves to scout around as far as might seem safe, and there was no danger of any surprise. There was one effect of all this even now to be seen in the sides of that stone wall. Windows had formed a part of the original plan, of course, but not nearly so many shot-holes.

"You see," said Jonas to Yellow Pine, "if any hostiles should ever make out to git inside the notch, this 'ere'd be the best kind of fort. Them holes are all big enough to poke a muzzle through."

"We'll have a stockade, some day," said Pine; "and we'll put another down at the gap, reg'lar fort fashion, with a gate and loop-holes."

Just then a whoop rang out from the braves at the gap and was followed by a chorus of them.

"I'd call it!" said Pine. "Knock off work, boys. Time's come."

Not quite, but a brave had ridden swiftly in with notice of the approach of the Apaches, and all the other scouts were fast following his good example. The first whoop had been given by the Big Tongue from behind the largest rocks of the barrier, but he was soon calmly walking up and down outside, as if waiting for the whole Apache nation, and also ready to be admired by somebody. One-eye was also beyond the barrier, for some reason, but he came in at the call of Two Arrows. There was no danger but what the Big Tongue would come in without any calling.

Na-tee-kah and Ha-ha-pah-no had done very little that morning but recite to their Nez Percé friends and relatives the wonders of their visit in the pale-face camp, and exhibit their rich store of ornaments and other presents. They had also combed and brushed each other's hair in a way that excited no little envy. They were yet busy at it when the voice of the Big Tongue was first heard at the barrier, and every squaw knew what it signified.

"Two Arrows," exclaimed Na-tee-kah, "has rifle now; kill heap."

"Big Tongue great brave," said Ha-ha-pah-no. "Shoot mouth; 'Pache heap die."

The horses, mules, and ponies of both Nez Percés and miners were all driven by the squaws away up the notch, under some trees, to be as secure as might be from stray bullets, if any should be fired. The squaws themselves were generally very willing to be as safe as were the animals; but Na-tee-kah's dusky cheeks were almost red with excitement. In spite of all prohibition, she broke away from under the trees and darted off towards the rocks on the side of the notch opposite the mine. It was only a minute before Ha-ha-pah-no followed her, with no idea of bringing her back, whatever she said to the rest on starting.

"See fight. Squaw shoot, too, sometime. Na-tee-kah heap brave."

Na-tee-kah did not utter a sound until she had gained a spot behind a huge bowlder, from which she could peer out and down, and see what was going on at the barrier and beyond it. She felt well paid for her trouble. The braves of the Nez Percés were all there or behind the rocky fragments on either side, and mingled with them here and there were the red shirts and slouched hats of the miners. The Big Tongue was no longer parading over the slope in front of the gap. He had even cut short an uncommonly fine whoop in his retreat to a place as safe as that occupied by Na-tee-kah or Ha-ha-pah-no.

There were excellent reasons for such a retreat, for several scores of Apaches were now riding back and forth, just out of good rifle-range, as if they were a little in doubt as to what they had better do next. Not an Apache among them had an idea how many might be the rifles among those rocks, but all were sure that they were there. It was just as Jonas had said, and Yellow Pine. It required an immense amount of courage to ride up to hidden sharpshooters, and the Apaches were disposed to whoop a good deal before they tried the experiment. Their head chief had commanded that there should be no random firing, and now he was disposed to try what could be done with a "talk." One solitary brave rode forward a distance in advance of his comrades, dismounted, laid down his rifle and lance, took off his pistol-belt ostentatiously, held up his hands wide open to declare himself unarmed, reached out his right hand with the palm up to say that he was peaceful, and then walked slowly forward.

"Wants to get near enough to see what he can see," said Yellow Pine. "Snake trick. I'll go out and meet him, jedge."

"No, Pine, I don't want you to run any risk."

"Risk? Not a bit of it. I say, Jonas, I'll let him come into good fair range. Keep him covered. If he tries any bad game I'll just drop flat."

"That's what he'll do next thing," said Jonas, as he rested his rifle over the log in front of him, and it seemed as if every other miner at once followed his example.

"Go ahead then, Pine," said the judge; "see what he wants."

"For that matter, jedge," said Pine, "I'd as lief as not try a hand-to-hand fight with any redskin in that lot."

He left his weapons behind him as ostentatiously as the Apache had done, handing them back over the barrier after stepping out, and walked forward rapidly, so that he did not let his conference turn into too close an "examination."

HIS RIGHT HAND WITH THE PALM UP TO SHOW THAT HE WAS PEACEFULToList

The keen eyes of the warrior were searching every cranny of the rocks as well as they could, when Yellow Pine drew near and held out his hand.

"How?" said Pine.

"How? Where Nez Percé?"

Pine answered by a sweep of his hand towards the notch, and added,

"'Pache chief want pony? want scalp? Go other place. Too much heap shoot; kill 'em all."

Chapter XXIX

STIRRING TIMES

The idea of a great fight about to come off had quite turned the heads of Sile and Two Arrows, and the later was aching all over with anxiety to try his new rifle. They had found good places to shoot from. Even the judge did not hesitate a moment about bidding Sile to do his duty, although he had a pretty strong conviction that there would not be much to do right away. Na-tee-kah had singled out that pair as the particular braves in whose conduct she was interested, but had no doubt that her brother would win more glory than the Red-head, now that he had so good a rifle.

The circumstances had even more completely turned the hot heads of the young Apache braves left in charge of their too numerous drove of horses. Every soul of them was crazy to be at the front and take part in whatever might turn up. They all seemed to drift naturally a little in that direction, and kept no kind of lookout, leaving their precious charge to take care of itself. The horses, therefore, at once began to take advantage of the grass.

This state of things continued, and grew worse and worse every minute, until a good long hour after the main body had moved away along Sile's trail towards the notch. Then, altogether unexpectedly, but as by one impulse, all the Apache horse-guard gave a sudden start and turned their heads in one direction.

Over the crest of the nearest knoll, stirring and clear and sweet, came the sound of a cavalry bugle. It was the signal to "charge," and was followed by the swift rush of Captain Grover and his men. In an instant they were between the feeding quadrupeds and their astonished keepers, and it was all in vain for the young hot-heads in their amazement to attempt to rally. One only wheeled his pony at once and rode away at the top of his speed. The nine or ten who dashed in the other direction suddenly all drew rein as they discovered the odds against them. A line of iron veterans, thirty strong, was thundering forward, and not an Apache was fool enough to fire a shot and be cut down for it.

There was just enough of bewildered, leaderless indecision to settle the matter. The sabres swept flashingly around the squad of redskins, and all they had to do was to surrender. It is a mere novelist's blunder to suppose and to write that red men have not sense enough to give it up when there is no use in fighting any more. They can do it as readily as any white man in the world, and the reason why they do not do it more frequently is because they generally keep a good chance to run away, and make a treaty afterwards as to what presents they are to have for making peace. There was no time given the young braves to strike a bargain. They were all disarmed, and then, dreadfully to their disgust, they were all dismounted and tied up.

"The plunder'll do well enough where it is," said Captain Grover, as he detailed Garry and a guard of four men to watch the prisoners. "If any of those chaps gets loose you'll have to shoot him. Men, by fours, left! Forward!"

The pony-rider who escaped was sure to carry the news of the disaster, and of the arrival of the blue-coats, but several things could happen before the Apache chief received it. He had no spy-glass, and he was eagerly waiting such information as might be obtained by the brave standing face to face with Yellow Pine.

That very cunning Apache found himself talking under difficulties. He could see distinctly that there were more than a few rifles at the barrier, but he could get no farther. The tall pale-face in front of him kept back any other information than that all the Apaches in this world or any other would be killed in case of an attack then and there. He even referred to Sile's exploit as an example, and to the lesson given by Two Arrows to the scout, and all the wild blood in the Apache brave was set boiling by that somewhat imprudent reference. He was a large, powerfully built warrior, and he had been as truthful as could be expected when he signified that he was unarmed. He kept up the idea of a "flag of truce" talk until sure he could gain no more by it, and then he uttered a shrill whoop and stooped, quick as a flash, for a long knife hidden in his leggings. He meant to carry back the scalp of Yellow Pine as a trophy of that conversation, but had not asked anybody how well Pine could box. The latter had no time to draw any weapon except his fist, but that was a hard one, and it struck the Apache on the side of his head as he was rising, knife in hand. Over and over he rolled, while Pine threw himself flat upon the earth, at the same moment digging both hands into the pockets of his pantaloons. His enemy recovered himself instantly and sprang to his feet with another whoop, lifting his long, glittering knife for a rush upon the prostrate pale-face. It might have been a perilous rush, for Pine's hands came right out of his pockets, and each held a short-barrelled "Derringer" pistol, ready cocked. They are terrible weapons, but the miner had no occasion to use either of them. The line of the barrier and of the adjacent rocks seemed to dance with blue flashes and with puffs of white smoke. Within three seconds not less than a score of rattling reports awoke the echoes of the notch, and every blue tube they came from had been aimed by a good marksman. After all was over, the prevalent opinion was that not one of them had missed. At all events Yellow Pine was safe to jump up and run for the barrier, followed by hasty shots from startled and galloping horsemen, all as useless as so many pebbles. His arrival was greeted by all the shouting and whooping which could possibly be performed by the red and white garrison of the notch, aided by One-eye with a vigor that shook him all over. Even then, however, the voice of the Big Tongue could be distinguished from the rest.

If the volume of sound did nothing else it deeply impressed the mind of the Apache chief with an idea of the strength of the force opposed to him. So had the promptness and number and accuracy of the rifle-shots which had prevented him from getting any report from his too treacherous "flag of truce" brave. As for him, Na-tee-kah had been watching Two Arrows and had seen the Apache fall just as his rifle went off. That was enough, and she was again proud of her brother. It was in vain for Ha-ha-pah-no to say,

"Ugh! Heap shoot. All kill him. Go dead a heap."

She as well as Na-tee-kah was taking every opportunity for practising all the small English words she could pick up, and some of her greatest successes would have puzzled a dictionary.

The Apaches were all but silent and drew back a little at the end of their burst of angry whooping and useless shooting. They drew back still farther because of a steady whizzing of bullets from the barrier. It was too far for good marksmanship, but the rifles made nowadays will send a piece of lead a mile and hurt something with it.

Suddenly a second burst of angry yells arose among the baffled marauders as a pony-rider in a great hurry dashed in among them, shouting forth the news of the arrival of the blue-coats and the loss of the drove and its protectors. Here was a blow indeed, and the escaped brave's estimate of the number of the cavalry he had run away from was very liberal. The Apache chief was necessarily a good captain, fully able to understand how bad it would be for him to be placed between two fires. The ground in front of the notch was therefore no place for him to fight in, and he did not know what precious minutes he had already been wasting. He threw away ten more in a sort of consultation with his wisest warriors, and at the same time his whole force rode up the valley a short distance. That move gave them the cover of some trees and took them out of range of bullets from the barrier, and at that very moment Judge Parks was startled by a yell from Sile.

"What are you doing up there?" he shouted, for Sile had clambered away up among the rocks of the lodge and stood upon a sort of pinnacle, spy-glass in hand.

"Cavalry, father! They are coming. Cavalry—"

"Come down!"

"Right in this direction. Riding hard. Hurrah!"

The new rifle of Two Arrows could not have won him the glory of that discovery and announcement. Once more the peculiar advantages of pale-faces over red men were forced upon him, but somehow it did but stir up his ambition, and with it a quick, daring impulse. He sprang away up the valley for a horse. He rushed in among the gathered animals of the corral, and boldly picked out his father's best and swiftest mustang, a beast that could run like the wind. He asked for no saddle, and the bridle went on as if by magic.

Sile came down from his perch at a rate that risked his neck, and made a report which drew from Yellow Pine,

"I'd call it—Jedge, if we could only let them fellers know we're here, it would be wuth a heap."

Before all who echoed that wish had finished speaking Two Arrows came dashing towards the barrier, all ready for the errand.

"Give the youngster three cheers!" shouted Yellow Pine. "Hurrah for him!"

CHAPTER XXX

A DARING RIDE

For the moment there was not one Apache horseman lingering within reach of the sharpshooters at the gap, and it was possible to get away from it unseen. All peril would come afterwards, but there was a vast amount of it, and the proposed errand of Two Arrows called for unlimited courage. His light weight upon a fresh racer gave him some advantage over heavy warriors upon horses already hard ridden, but this fact did not cover the whole question by any means, for a bullet will travel faster than the swiftest mustang. Sile did his best to communicate every fact that his spy-glass had given him; Long Bear said "Ugh!" with a deep and expressive intonation; the logs were removed from the entrance; and then Na-tee-kah's heart beat terribly, for she saw her hero brother dash forth all alone, she could not guess why nor whither. Then there was another sudden commotion, for Yellow Pine shouted, and Long Bear echoed it in his own tongue,

"Mount, men! Mount and be ready, every mother's son of ye! I'm jest going to back that there young catamount if it costs me my hair!"

There was the swiftest kind of saddling and mounting, and not a Nez Percé boy old enough to draw a bow was willing to be left behind. When, therefore, the whole force rode out upon the slope in front of the notch, it looked a good deal stronger than it really was. All that work required many minutes, and during all of these the daring young messenger had been doing capitally.

Leaving the gap, he wheeled his fleet mustang to the right and dashed away until he deemed himself within reach of a small grove of trees, around which he could sweep back into the right course to reach the cavalry. It was an acute enough calculation, but out of that very bit of bushy timber came first a brace of rifle-bullets and then a pair of mounted Apaches, as soon as these believed that they had let him go far enough. That is, they rode out to cut off his return, and they both failed to do him or his horse any harm. It was a race now, with the chances against the pursuers, and Two Arrows sent back a derisive whoop as he struck out straight for what he believed to be his mark. He understood in an instant that he had escaped the main body of his enemies, but there was no telling when he might meet one of their smaller squads. He felt in every fibre of his body that he was now armed as a warrior, and was doing the work of a warrior and of an uncommonly daring brave. His heart beat with fierce delight and hope, and his very mustang seemed to feel the excitement, and went forward with long, eager bounds. The wind was in his face, and now it brought him something. It was a faint sound, and far away, but it was the bugle-note which bade Captain Grover's men to change their trot to a gallop.

The little force of cavalry had taken upon them no small risk in dashing forward, now that they had a better knowledge of the strength of their opponents. It was almost rashness, but it was such a facing of odds as our gallant soldiers are all the while doing. There was nothing exceptional about it, terrible as have been the disasters now and then resulting. Captain Grover determined to gain whatever might be gained by promptly following up his first success, and so he had well used all the minutes the Apache chief was wasting. At about the time when the latter had decided that there must be an effort made to recover the lost plunder, unless the cavalry should prove too numerous, Captain Grover had ridden far enough to make good the military plan of a young Nez Percé chief. His own spy-glass was at work from every rising ground he came to, and now it brought an exclamation from him:

"What's up now? One chased by two? Forward! Gallop!"

Two Apache braves, already very sure they could not catch the rider they were chasing, wheeled quickly and rode in the opposite direction, and in a few moments more Two Arrows was rapidly explaining the situation to Captain Grover. It was a very plain one, and not a second was wasted in considering it. Again the word was "forward," and the remaining distance to be travelled was not great. The decision of the Apaches to advance was likely to make it shorter, but that was an unpleasant time for the chief in command of those unlucky red men. Just as two of his braves came in to inform him that a messenger from the men among the rocks had reached the cavalry, another announced that all the pale-faces and Nez Percés had come out from the rocks to fight and were "heap strong." Nor was that the whole of it, for one of his scouts from the rear dashed up with the news that yet another party of Nez Percés was coming, he did not know how many. These were the fellows sent through the pass for the "cached" property, but what Apache could say how many more might follow? or how many more blue-coated veterans might be at hand?

It looked for all the world as if that enterprising band of Apache "business men" were surrounded and trapped. They had already lost all the proceeds of their season's hard work, and the rest of their stock in trade, of all sorts, was pretty sure to follow. More consultation was absolutely necessary, and before it was over Sile could announce, from his perch upon the rock,

"Coming! I can see Two Arrows."

Then there was a cheering, and Na-tee-kah felt all but proud of the noise made by the Big Tongue—there was so very much of it.

"Forward, men!" shouted Judge Parks. "We must be on hand. Come down, Sile. Keep near *me*."

Sile was down and mounted in a moment, but there was to be no great battle that day. The Apache "council of war" lasted until it could hear the cavalry bugle and the distant whoop of the Big Tongue. It could not hear the howl of One-eye, for that brave animal was sitting in the very entrance of the barrier guarding the notch, all alone except for the squaws. It was better to go upon any reservation, and to promise any amount and degree of good behavior, than to spend the remainder of that fine day in being shot and sabred. So the council decided, and so, in due and dignified form, they announced to Captain Grover, before he had an opportunity to bid his veterans charge.

The official duty of the captain, after that, was to disarm his captives, the weapons to be all returned upon reaching the reservation, and to order them at once into a camp by themselves, under a guard. Word was sent to Garry and his men to move the quadrupeds down the river as fast as possible, the prisoners there being untied and sent to their main body. Rapid orders were given, and were mingled with as rapid conversations with Judge Parks, Yellow Pine, and Long Bear.

"Where's that messenger?" suddenly exclaimed Captain Grover, after he had listened to the facts as to the sending of Two Arrows. There was a glow upon the brave soldier's face, and he was unbuckling the flap of one of his holsters, for he was yet in the saddle.

Two Arrows was summoned and came forward, and a great many eyes were upon him.

"Young brave!" said Captain Grover emphatically. "I never heard of a pluckier volunteer in all my life. Take that; keep your head level, that's all. You've more courage than you've any real need of."

"That" was a handsome silver-mounted army revolver. Given in that way it was a mark of distinction for a great chief to be proud of, and Long Bear, indeed, was nearly as proud as was Two Arrows.

"There, Sile," said his father; "see that you do as well with your advantages as that Nez Percé boy has done with his."

"I will, father; but why could he not have some more? What is to hinder him from going to school? There's all my gold, now, in the wagon; I'd spend a good deal of it."

"Sile, my boy, I've been thinking of it. We will do it. It's a good thing. The girl too."

It was time now for Captain Grover to ride in and see the notch and the mine, and to get the best dinner the miners and Ha-ha-pah-no could cook for him and his men. Then it was time for Na-tee-kah to go nearly wild with pride over her brother and his revolver. After that there was a long consultation between Long Bear and his children and Judge Parks and Sile. Two Arrows seemed to be inclined to say very little at first. He sat with his new rifle across his lap, and his priceless revolver resting upon that, and One-eye came and sat down beside him. Long Bear himself seemed to be in doubt as his pale-face friends urged upon him the advantages of their offer. He was hardly able to see what good there could be in the learning of the white men for a red horseman of the plains; but at last Two Arrows motioned to Sile for his spy-glass, hanging at his side. He took it and looked through it at the distant mountains, and then turned to Long Bear and pointed at them, saying,

"Look! See!"

"Ugh!" said the old chief, "see heap."

"Now look. See," said Two Arrows, "see big heap."

"Ugh! Big medicine," said Long Bear, handing the glass to Sile, but Two Arrows arose and stood proudly erect, rifle in hand.

"Will you go?" asked Sile.

"Go," said Two Arrows. "Good friend. Go. Got Nez Percé eye now; want pale-face eye."

"Ugh!" exclaimed Long Bear; "what Na-tee-kah say?"

The question was put to her, but it was hardly needful, after she found that Two Arrows was to go. She was willing to learn anything he did, and she was not even daunted by quick mental vision of a white lady with her bonnet on. She would even wear the dress of a pale-face squaw if Two Arrows would put on such things as were worn by the Red-head. So it was settled, although it would be a number of weeks before the judge and Sile could set out for their eastern home.

At several points in the East there are schools designed and maintained for the special education of Indian girls and boys, only needing greater help from men and women who have money intrusted to them by the Giver.

Among all the tribes of the West, and in every band, Na-tee-kah and Two Arrows wait to be found and enticed into a training that is for their everlasting good and for that of their race.

THE END